CAPTURED

He captured her homestead;
she captured his heart.

An Inspirational Historical Romance

Novel by Award Winning Author

Eva Maria Hamilton

Bible quotes taken from the New King James Version.

Cover Design by Eva Maria Hamilton

This is a work of fiction. Names, characters, places, and incidents, are either the product of the author's imagination or are used fictitiously, and any resemblance to actual persons, living or dead, business establishments, events or locales is entirely coincidental.

ISBN: 978-1-0689907-0-0

http://www.LilacLanePublishing.com

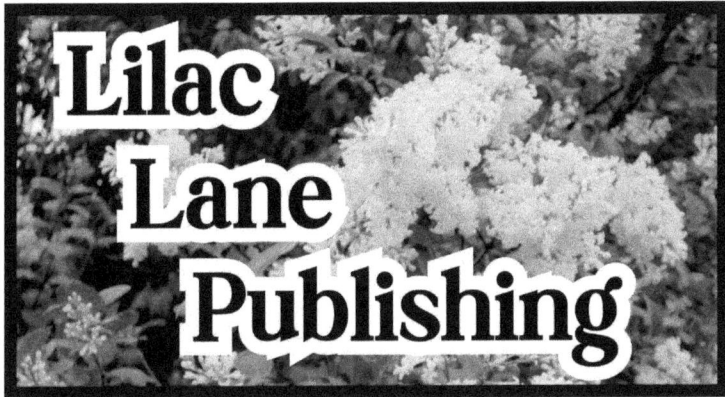

Dedicated with all my love to my family, especially my husband, Jason; daughters, Michelina and Angelina; collies, Daisy and Glory; parents, Bob and Lina; and brother, Bill.

I thank God for blessing me with you, along with all the other exceptional people He has placed in my life.

With special thanks to everyone who entered my Name The Hero Contest, especially Jenny Blake who won, Amy Knupp of Blue Otter for her initial critique, and Brenda Minton who also shared a bit of her expertise with me a decade ago when this book was born. Also, thank you to Harlequin for releasing the rights of my characters from Highland Hearts back to me so this series could come to life.

A time to love, and a time to hate; a time of war, and a time of peace. — Ecclesiastes 3:8

Queenston, Upper Canada

Wednesday, June 23, 1813

During the War of 1812

*F*iona Robertson's hands shook. The money she held dropped to the floor. She glanced at her bedroom window, but she couldn't see past the sun's piercing rays. Squinting away from the brightness, she swooped down, retrieved the money, and jammed it into her sack. A roar of thunder assaulted her ears. But the noise had not arisen from a rainstorm. This variety, brewed from a gravely different source.

She grabbed her empire waist gown, lifted her skirts, and ran from the room. In her rush, she traversed the stairs too quickly and slipped down the last few steps. She didn't allow that to slow her pace though as she dashed into the drawing room.

Flinging herself onto the floor, she clawed at the braided oval rug until she had tugged it back to expose the loosened floorboard underneath.

Her fingers wrenched off the plank of wood and she threw her sack into the hidden compartment that she had made nearly a year ago, when the American's had declared war on the

British and hence her colony in Upper
Canada.

*God, please assure they pass me
by. So far, You've kept me safe as war
has waged around me, especially last
month when the Americans seized Fort
George.*

The thunder grew louder and she
doubted that this time God could keep
her out of harm's way. Nevertheless,
she thanked Him for giving her the
foresight to liquidate her valuables.
She had to hide her meager wealth. Her
dream of breeding horses needed to
remain intact. She had worked too long
and hard to allow her dream to die.

She slammed the wooden plank back
down, stood, and kicked the rug
overtop to conceal it. *God, please
protect me.* She grabbed hold of a
chair for support as the rumble
approached.

Perhaps they shan't come to her
remote homestead. They had never
ventured on her land thus far and
hardly ever even bothered with the
people of Queenston. They may just be
marching through on their way to
another battle.

A deep voice, in the distance, shouted something indiscernible. Her eyes darted about the room. Her sofa, thin tea table with twin chairs, narrow games table for two, and rickety writing desk did not offer anywhere to hide.

Her breath stilled as a shadow crossed her window. She scurried from the room. But a thump on her entrance door flattened her against the white, unadorned vestibule wall.

Another bang jolted her head to the right. She watched the wood rattle beside her under each new beating. Soon 'twould be knocked clear off its hinges.

Tremors rocked her body. And her hands flew up to shield her face as the massive wooden door hurtled toward her.

Men marched into her passageway—American soldiers.

Nay, God. Not here. Not in my home.

She didn't move. She didn't even dare breathe as the men invaded her private sanctuary. Banging, crashing,

ripping—the sounds of pillaging
wrought her nerves.

She must flee.

With frantic fingers clutched to
the door, she slid along its width
toward the open air. One more step and
she could run.

A hand seized her arm. "Unhand
me!" She struggled.

The American jerked her back in.
"We need someone to cook for us whilst
we stay here."

Stay here? Her arm fell limp. She
couldn't fight this man off, and even
if she could, he had come with a whole
regiment, she couldn't fight them all.

Another crash, louder than the
others, diverted the American's
attention. She tugged her arm free.
Without pause, she turned and ran.

Her hair lifted with the speed of
her steps, but it dropped dead when
she ploughed directly into a human
wall.

Two hands gripped her shoulders
and steadied her as air refilled her
lungs. She kept her head down and the
man barked orders over her, "Halt. I
shan't permit such behavior. Whilst

we're here, you shall honor this home as if it were your own. We're Americans. Let's conduct ourselves accordingly. We didn't begin this war to oppress anyone."

The chaos immediately ceased as the man who still held her commanded authority. "To-day ought to have been a day for rest, but alas, you've thrown this house into disarray, and hence, setting things right shall be your first priority."

As the soldiers began to settle in, the man dropped his hands from her shoulders. "I apologize for any damage. There's no excuse for their behavior. And I shall see to it that no one acts disrespectfully from here onward."

She bit her cheek. She had heard stories that even the British soldiers were taking terrible liberties just as these Americans had. But here stood a man, fighting against her country, that didn't wish his men to commit the horrible atrocities that had become so common in this war.

She owed him, and God, her gratitude. "Thank you." Her eyes

locked on his face as he dipped his
chin. She stepped back. The man before
her exuded an incredible presence. And
yet, he seemed familiar
somehow—something about his rich
brown eyes.

"Please oblige me by stepping out
of doors so I may speak with you?" The
stoicism departed from his handsome
face. She nodded and followed him out.

She tensed when he stopped
suddenly and she almost bumped into
his musket. "Again, I do apologize on
behalf of my men for behaving so
recklessly." The man turned to face
her. "If circumstances had not held me
back, I'd have been here to prevent
such an abrupt and destructive
intrusion. The younger lads become a
wee—" He looked off into the distance
at the Niagara River.

But she kept her mouth shut, she
couldn't agree. The American who had
grabbed her arm was roughly the same
age and rank as the man before her and
he hadn't objected to any of the
soldiers' behavior.

"Do you reside on this homestead
alone?" She bit her lip and dipped her

chin slightly. "Do you not have a husband?" She shook her head. "Any kinfolk?"

"Nay." She dropped her gaze to the man's black gaiters. No husband. No family. Only her, and God, and a homestead full of animals, including a Quarter Horse, on whom she had staked all her dreams for the future.

"That places us in a precarious predicament." The man leaned on his musket. "We cannot allow you to run off, and yet, you cannot remain in a house full of soldiers." Hotness rose to her cheeks. "And before you seek to inquire, I may be able to maintain your safety, but I cannot refuse my men a comfortable night's rest."

She looked away at a small wooden building a little beyond her stone water-well. "I can sleep in my store." She pointed. "'Tis just over yonder."

"Splendid. That shall be one less problem." The man seemed to work down a list in his head. "I shall accompany you to retrieve your things." She merely looked at him. "After you." He swung his arm out.

"Um—" she rubbed her hands "—I'd rather not lead, if 'tis all the same to you."

The man bowed his head. "Certainly. Please, follow me." He strode into her home and pinned looks on any soldiers that happened to glance in their direction.

Heavy footsteps plodded up the stairs before he ducked to save his head from hitting her slanted ceiling. With sturdy strides, he crossed the few feet it took to enter her newly disheveled bedroom. The soldiers within fell silent and she shuddered at the thought of them having foraged through her things.

"Men, this woman requires privacy?" They filed out and she was left to stare at the powerful man.

He stared back, his jaw set, and shoulders squared with mountainous muscles threatening to tear through his uniform.

She swallowed. "Please, do spare me a moment?"

"Of course." He grinned sheepishly, and something about his

smile threw her mind back to when she had been a youth. "Are you unwell?"

"Nay." She shook the thoughts away, but he hesitated before he stepped out.

With a deep breath, she watched him adopt a posture that showed he stood fully on guard as he remained in sight with his back to her. She rubbed her bruised arm. Actually, now that she thought of it, aye, she most certainly was *unwell*. Her homestead had just been captured by Americans!

However, she grimaced, it could have been worse. Much worse. She pulled her eyes off the impressive man and appraised her small bedroom. Her pitcher and washbasin lay on the floor. The table they usually sat on was overturned. Her chamber pot chair had been kicked sideways, and her rocking chair moved back and forth as if to comfort itself.

To shut out the mayhem, she bent to retrieve her valise from under the bed. With more strength than she needed, she flung it on top of the jumbled blankets that lay on her straw mattress. Opening the case, she inadvertently unleashed another myriad of memories.

She hadn't used this traveling receptacle in eighteen years, not since she moved here to live with her aunt. But she shan't allow her mind to return to when she was fifteen. And definitely not before then, when she still had her mother, father, and brother.

She picked up the bundle of dried lavender that lay within and squeezed her eyes shut. The sweet scent coursed through her as a reminder of her aunt's fondness for flowers. Her aunt must have stowed the bouquet in there, years ago, before she and her uncle died.

She tucked the lavender back inside with a prayer for the departed, and quickly turned to rummage through what remained in her lone bureau, before she gathered her discarded clothes from the floor. She ought not dally.

"I've finished." She dropped her valise off the bed and began to drag it toward the door.

"Allow me." The man didn't wait for her consent. He bent his head low, marched forward, and plucked the case from her as if it weighed nothing more than a chicken.

"Thank you," she murmured, with a final look at her bedroom, which wouldn't be truly hers again, for who knew how long—or, if ever.

She stepped into the passageway, somewhat relieved they didn't encounter any soldiers as they proceeded to exit the house. Where the other men were and what they did, she knew not, because besides shooting muskets to kill across a battlefield, she knew little else about what soldiers did.

"Do you actually possess the time to accompany me?" she asked. After all, he did indeed appear to be the only American who seemed to care.

"I shall make the time." He led them to her store and set her valise down, then stepped out of the way to give her room to unlock the door.

But she had slowed her pace, this was the last part of her homestead that the American soldiers hadn't damaged and she didn't wish any of them near her merchandise.

Under his watchful eye, she fumbled with the key. Finally, she resigned with a sigh. Her attempt to stall was pointless. If these soldiers wished to enter her store, a wee encumbrance like a lock ought not to deter them.

"Do you possess everything you need to be comfortable in here?" The man carried her receptacle in and placed it atop the sole table in the middle of the room.

She stood in the doorway, annoyed as his eyes swept over her shelves lined with goods. "I shall be fine." Her teeth clenched.

"This is indeed striking." His hand swept over a square quilt that lay on the table. "Does the credit for this handiwork belong to you?"

"Aye." She crossed her arms. "I stictched it this past winter."

"Did you design the pattern yourself?"

"Nay." She shifted her weight to rest on her left leg. Why was this military man so interested in a quilt?

"I emulated that medallion pattern from a quilt my mother stictched whenst I was a wee lass."

The man's gaze shot to hers. Her body ached to squirm under his intense scrutiny. But she willed herself to remain like a statue.

He moved toward her and his sudden nearness stopped the air flow to her lungs. She squared herself in the doorway.

His eyes searched hers. "Fiona?" Her name, from his lips, stopped her heart. Who was this American?

"How is it you know my name?"

Shock registered on his face, only to be torn apart by a grin that stretched the length of it. "Fiona Robertson?"

She nodded. "Do I know you?"

He laughed. Moisture clutched his orbs. "I should hope so. I thought I recognized you the moment you ran into me. However, given how much time has passed, I conceded to my uncertainty."

He bowed, and took her hand up to his lips. His touch was gentle and the unexpected kiss sent a shiver up her spine. Without releasing her, his eyes returned to hers. "Allow me to remind you. I'm Lachlan McAllister."

She gasped. "Little Lock-Me-Up?" And that grin that had caused her to stop and take notice of him arose once more on his face. She ought to have recognized him before he told her his name. Those features. That brown hair. The brown eyes. All the McAllister men had those same attributes.

Her head spun. The man before her was no stranger. He had been her deceased brother's best friend.

Fiona. Her name alone sounded akin to a song in Lachlan's head. He thought the lass his boyhood heart had dreamt of marrying had been lost to him forever. But here she stood, and he couldn't take his eyes off her.

"Seeing as you're a military man, I suppose the nickname we bestoed upon you is no longer befitting." Her full lips spread upward into a smile. "Little Lock-Me-Up." She shook her head of light brown hair.

He chuckled. "If you truly did expect me to mature into a criminal,

I've gravely disappointed you by becoming an officer."

A captivating sparkle shone in her hazel eyes. "As my late brother's best friend, I'm glad to witness you've chosen a good path in life. It makes me happy to assume that had my brother lived he ought not to have been led into a world of mischief."

He shrugged. "I suppose. Although, perhaps had he lived, 'tis I who'd have been the one led into that sort of life. Your brother, God rest his soul, was most certainly a rascal. Allbeit, a noble one."

She smiled. "I cannot deny it." A tear fell from her eye and she wiped it away with the knuckle of her right forefinger. "You were inseparable. And he never seemed bereft of an extraordinary tale to share regarding one of your feats. He loved you as a brother, Lachlan. Truly, he did."

He nodded. He knew. The death of his best friend had severed his heart. "I do indeed think of him often."

"I do, as well." She clasped her hands together in front of her light green gown.

"I'm sorry." He stepped in and rubbed her arm. The same exhilaration he felt as a lad rolled through him and he snatched his hand away.

He ought not to have touched her anyway. If any of the soldiers had seen him and mistook the situation—for one, he was not that sort of man, and two, he'd turn on his own men if they took any liberties with her.

"Thank you." She stepped out of the store's entryway, and into the morning sun. "As the sister of your deceased best friend, may I please inquire as to what shall become of me and my homestead?" She looked out over her land.

"You mustn't refer to me as merely your deceased brother's friend." He stood behind her, fingers squeezed into the barrel of his musket. "I was your friend, as well."

Her gaze met his, and knowing eyes bored into him as if she could read his thoughts. He swallowed hard. He had never told her exactly how he had felt about her.

She shuffled past him and locked the store's door. "I must confess—" her gown flew into a flurry of movement as she spun to face him "—I'm scared." The honesty of her utterance fractured something deep inside him.

He strode toward her. "Before I realized exactly who you were, I told you I shan't allow any harm to befall you. And I meant it." However, now that he knew her identity, those feelings had heightened. Before anyone harmed her, they'd have to kill him first.

Her lips tipped up in the corners. "I cannot express what a comfort it is to have you here. I've already thanked God so much, I'm certain He's tired of my voice."

He smiled, but it soon faded. "I hope you understand, I cannot tell you anything specific. You're a British citizen now. I cannot divulge any of the information I know."

She nodded, but it irked him not to be able to talk to her freely. He did indeed wish to ease her fears.

Taking a deep breath, he released it just as slowly, then lowered his voice, "You shan't be required to cook too many meals for us." He stared at her, hoping she grasped his meaning. His regiment shan't remain here long.

She took his hand and squeezed it. "Thank you." Her somber expression revolted into a smile. "So I must in fact feed all of you?"

His nose crinkled. "Aye."

She bit her lower lip. "Pray tell, what shall become of me if the soldiers don't fancy my fare?"

"Fret not. There have been many a day where we've gone hungry, hence anything eatable is sure to delight."

"I pray you're correct, because I truly don't wish to discover otherwise." She tucked a stray strand of hay colored hair behind her ear. "I still have yet to fed my animals their breakfast though, and I must feed them before I set about preparing dinner for a whole regiment of American soldiers."

"Of course." He lifted his musket to rest on his shoulder as he stepped aside to allow her to lead. "Permit me to walk you to them."

"Thank you." She picked up the light green material of her gown with one hand and hurried forward.

Fiona looked toward the barn. "My animals must be nearing starvation by now." Her lightheartedness dissipated and her whole body went rigid once she saw that not only was the barn door open, but two soldiers stood in the entrance, whilst her farm collie, Scolty, growled at them from within.

"Nay, Scolty. Enough." But the dog had already snapped at a soldier and barred his teeth at the other. *God, please prohibit these soldiers from silencing my dearest companion.* She ran to her dog's side. "Please, he's not accustomed to strangers." She grabbed Scolty's collar. "This is his home. Surely you must appreciate that he's merely guarding his territory."

The soldiers didn't retreat and perspiration beaded on her forehead.

"Men, please inform the others that dinner shall be served at one

o'clock." The soldiers nodded at
Lachlan, then abruptly left.

Her shoulders slumped. She owed
him even more thanks. But her
gratitude must wait. She'd be unable
to voice her thanks over Scolty's
growl. "Nay. Enough, Scolty." She
squeezed her fingers tighter around
his collar. "He still perceives you as
a threat. Please refrain from coming
any closer."

With his eyes fixed on her dog,
he conducted himself in a manner
completely opposite to her warning.
"Scolty." He pulled out a piece of
bread, from one of the many bags he
had slung across his body. He held it
out to her dog. "Scolty", he called
again, as he approached with an
emanating calmness.

Her dog's collar tugged less
under her fingers, until his snarl
ceased and he began to sniff the air.
"Come, Scolty. Come here." He stopped
a few feet away, still holding out the
bread. "Here's food."

She loosened her hand around her
dog's collar, sucked in a breath and
held it. When his tail finally

swished, she let him go. He took
several cautious steps toward Lachlan,
reached out his neck and took the
food, then ate it, as if she hadn't
fed him since last week.

"Good, dog." He took his time
drawing out another piece of bread.
And she finally exhaled. She didn't
dare speak though, knowing any sudden
movement could break her dog's trust
in him.

With slow, controlled precision,
he held the bread closer to his body
and drew her dog closer to him. When
he did it once more, he patted
Scolty's head.

"He loves you now." She scratched
her dog's back, as he fed him another
piece of bread. "You've gone and
spoiled him."

He smiled up at her. The lad she
had known had definitely kept his
ability to charm. But thinking of him
in such terms sent a heat to her
cheeks. "I better set about my work, I
have animals to feed."

"Aye." He stood, giving her dog
another pat on the head. "And not just

in here. The men shall be hungry come one o'clock."

She chuckled. "Are you to dine, as well?"

"I most certainly am. I shan't dream of missing your dinner." He winked at her, and that sent her heart into a full gallop.

Although understanding such a reaction to him, she could not. He had been her brother's best friend. Her *younger* brother. She had never thought of him as a potential beau before. But hide it from herself she could no longer—her thoughts had most definitely veered in that direction. Even despite the fact that he fought on the American side of this war and shan't even be here much longer.

"If I'm able, I shall look in on you before dinner." He replaced his black shako hat on his head. She nodded. "Remember not to exert yourself. The men aren't particular. And besides, I shan't wish you overworked."

"I shall attempt to remember that." She pulled her lips into the faintest smile. But work, hard work,

exhausting work that sent her to bed
every night unable to move from
stiffness had been the only life she
had known since her aunt and uncle had
died.

"Good." He hesitated. Did he wish
to say something more? The depths of
his caramel eyes carried plenty of
meaning, but after all these years,
she stood as no expert on the man. And
man he was. She had known the lad, not
this, six foot something, handsome
officer. "Until dinner." He dipped his
chin.

"Aye." She watched him march
away.

*   *   *

"There, Big Bonnie, the last of
your food." Fiona rubbed her white
pig's head. "Sorry for my tardiness."
The sow devoured her breakfast and she
ran her hand over the swine's wiry
hairs. "Enjoy your mud in the yard
later, it shall be another hot day."
The hog snorted, as she put her pail
away before she trudged out of the
barn toward the house to begin dinner.

"Fiona, Fiona!" her name crackled through the air before she spotted her neighbor bustling toward her.

She stopped, and squeezed her hands together. But she didn't wince, a sharp tongue that loved to gossip shan't unnerve her to-day, not after her homestead had been invaded by Americans. "Good morning, Mrs. Johnson."

The out of breath matron scowled at her words while she pinched her side. *"Good morning*? I dare say this morning has been anything but *good*." She couldn't disagree. "Has yer home been taken over by those ghastly American soldiers?" She nodded, which produced a gasp from Mrs. Johnson. "Oh dear, what shall ye do? Ye're all alone out here. 'Tis an abomination." Her head shook most vehemently. "Why an unwed woman, like yerself, with a house full of men, 'tis sure to cause speculation. Ye'll be ruined."

"I shall be in my store—alone," she took advantage of the smallest break in the woman's rant to enlighten her. "I assure you nothing untoward has happened, and I've been guaranteed nothing shall." She crossed her arms to emphasize her point.

"I pray, fer yer sake, 'tis true, but ye know how people talk." She bit her tongue. She did indeed know how those akin to Mrs. Johnson lived to gossip. "I wonder if my home shall ever be the same." The woman pulled at her grey bonnet that matched her pelisse. "And 'tis not merely us." She brought her hand down, waving it about. "The entire town of Queenston is under these Americans. I just snuck to Laura's homestead and she's suffering the same fate. Her entire house has been pillaged and all her belongings have either been destroyed or stolen. Those knaves. There are American soldiers everywhere."

She continued to throw her hand about, until it finally rested on her hip. "Now mind ye, Laura and I have husbands, so we shan't be speculated against. But ye—" she snorted "—oh dear, what is to become of ye now?"

She unclenched her fingers that had dug into the wincey fabric of her gown. "I shall be just fine." She folded her hands together in front of her.

"I cannot fathom how." The woman's stern black brows pulled together. "Perhaps ye should seek the doctor's help. He may be able to offer a solution to yer lodging problems. He's—"

"Nay." She'd never—ever—ask the town doctor for anything.

"Fiona, ye must be reasonable, my young cousin, Edgar—"

"Thank you for your concern, Mrs. Johnson." She dropped her hands to her sides. "I do hope the American soldiers who invaded your home do not completely destroy it. But I simply cannot stay and converse any longer. I have an entire regiment of soldiers expecting a dinner that I have yet to cook."

"Well, then," she huffed. "Good day to ye. I hope ye're in God's favor enough for Him to keep ye safe."

She pasted on a smile. "You, as well."

Mrs. Johnson inhaled sharply, raised her nose in the air, and then stomped away.

She took a deep breath, shook her head, and then plodded home. She didn't wish to spend another minute thinking about what may have occurred earlier if Lachlan hadn't been here.

A faint smile rose to her cheeks when she spotted him marching directly toward her in his blue and white uniform—that he filled out flawlessly. He performed every movement with an exactness that he had perfected in his one and thirty years.

"How do the dinner preparations progress?" He moved his musket from one shoulder to the other as he fell into step with her.

"I'm just about to commence with them." She glanced sideways at him.

His lips curled. "Care to tell a hungry officer what I may anticipate?"

"I fear I shall only have time to prepare biscuits and soup. But I promise the broth shall be hearty for I shall add chicken, rice, flour, and vegetables."

His lips tugged upward even farther. "Now I most definitely shall be incapable of focusing on anything until I sample your fare."

With a shake of her head she smiled. He was kind and sweet, but she knew not how the other Americans would react. Tension knotted her stomach.

"Do you need me to procure the chickens?" he asked.

She stalled. She hadn't had anyone on her homestead to help her for some time now. "Do you mean to shoot them?"

He let out an unbridled laugh. "I don't shoot my musket unless 'tis absolutely necessary." He tipped his hat toward her, with a wink that broadened her smile.

However, her good humor disappeared the moment she heard gunpowder explode.

Eva Maria Hamilton

Lachlan felt Fiona's hands clutch his arm. Her closeness ignited a surge of defense that streaked through his blood. Torn, he wished to remain here to guard her, and yet, he knew he must investigate

30

those musket shots. If the British had attacked, he must fight.

Another explosion ripped through the air. She clung closer to his side. "Fiona, please, take yourself indoors and fasten the lock. Stay away from your windows and don't allow anyone to enter."

The look of terror in her eyes bore into his heart. She didn't belong anywhere near a battlefield.

"Promise to be careful?" She remained close. Her clean scent wafted up to him, and beckoned him not to tear himself away.

"I shall." He moved her away from him. "Now please, take yourself indoors."

She hesitated a moment, then ran. When the door slammed shut behind her, he changed his sights to the battle before him and marched out to meet it.

Fiona did exactly as Lachlan had instructed. She sat huddled in the corner of her bedroom, her hands clasped in prayer that he'd return unharmed.

Deep in her attempt to turn her worries over to the Lord, she jumped when she heard a bang on the door downstairs.

Unsteady limbs scrambled up the side of the wall, yet hope rose in her chest—Lachlan had returned. She ran, but stopped in the doorway as his words of caution whirled through her mind. Her breathing faltered. She clutched the doorframe. What if the person who had knocked wasn't him?

She held her breath to listen. She didn't hear anything besides her heart pounding in her chest, and she couldn't see who had knocked. She crept down the stairs.

Another bang shook her backdoor. Her feet soldered themselves to the wood floor.

But suppose the caller was another woman, or a child, who sought refuge. Dread seized her. She must see who stood on the other side of that door.

"Fiona, 'tis I. Please, open the—" Lachlan's last word caught in his throat as the door swung open and her body slammed into his.

"Oh, Lachlan." She hugged him tight. "I thought you may have been injured." His body melted into hers and he held her tighter as she shook under him.

But he couldn't hold her forever. She didn't belong to him. And this was not the time to start wooing her. "Everything is fine." He loosened his hold on her.

She pulled farther away, her face still creased with worry. "Are you certain? Who was responsible for the shootings?"

He grinned and took her hand. "Come with me." She followed him without voicing a single question, and her complete trust in him warmed him. He may be the enemy on paper, but 'twas clear that their shared past hadn't disappeared from her mind either.

Leading her around the corner of her one and a half storey house, she tightened her grip at the sight of blood, then a laugh escaped her lips.

"I suppose I shan't need you to fetch me any chickens for dinner."

He nodded. "Some of the men required shooting practice."

"That explains the noise." She surveyed the pile of dead squirrels.

"I shall bring these in for you." He picked up the carcasses and followed her into the kitchen. At the far left side of the room, in front of a large window, he set the uncooked meat down on her wooden table.

She stopped in the middle of the kitchen and took an extremely large black iron pot off her hearth's crane. "I' shall fill that with water whilst you start the fire," he insisted.

"I'm more than capable of accomplishing both tasks." Her head tipped sideways. "I am accustomed to it."

"I don't doubt your ability. And I apologize if I've overstepped my welcome. But I'd rather it be me here than one of the soldiers. I hope you shall allow me help you whilst I am here." She handed him the pot and he flashed her a smile. "And besides, my mother, not to mention my grandmother, would be appalled if I failed to assist you."

That brought the corner of her lips up. "I shan't ever wish to cause a moments trouble on that front." She stepped back toward the hearth and turned her back to him. He stayed only long enough to see her long hair sway behind her.

Fiona stacked wood in the hearth whilst tears cascaded down her cheeks. Her uncle had never allowed her to fetch water either. How she missed him, and her aunt, and the warmth and courteousness that being surrounded by a loving family afforded.

With the fire lit, she stood, she must not allow her mind to wander any further back, especially to when her parents lived and they all inhabited their cozy home in the Mohawk Valley of the United States.

She took a deep breath.

Knowing she needed to banish these thoughts, she traipsed out of the house. The June heat hung almost unbearable as she stood just beyond the door to compose herself.

"Lachlan, 'tis the bucket that's supposed to traverse the well, not you." She laughed at the distraction his soaking wet hair caused as water dripped down his blue coat and onto his white overalls.

With a huge grin, he shook his head when he neared her. Water droplets flew through the air. She held her hands in front of her. "Stop!" She backed up and fled to the kitchen. "Not all of us retain such a fine appearance whilst soaked like wet dogs." She bit her lip. Too late. She had just revealed she thought him handsome.

"As I recall, water never soured your beauty." He removed his gaze from her to hang the pot over the fire. She walked straight to the table, determined not to allow him to see her cheeks flame red. "Do you remember the old pond, Fiona?"

Her hands stilled. She felt his presence beside her. "Certainly." She didn't look at him and forced herself to chop the meat. "I still dream about growing up in New Callander, and the time I spent at the pond with you and my brother are the memories that put an immediate smile upon my face."

"'Tis still there." His breath moved across her neck as he went to sit on the wooden chair at the head of the table. "At least the last time I was home."

She glanced over to see him snatch up a towel that had lain on the table. "How long have you been away?"

"Approximately, one year." He wiped his wet hands before he folded the towel and set it back down.

"A year? Do you not miss your family?"

Eyes the color of chocolate met hers. "Aye. But this is the career I've chosen, so these are the terms I must live with. Being an officer is important to me and I have to see this war to the end."

"Even if it *ends* your life?" She held his gaze.

"Aye." His back straightened. "Men have died much less honorable deaths." His chest lifted with a sharp intake of breath. "However, I do pray every night that this war shall cease shortly."

"I pray for that, as well." She plunked some meat into a bowl, before cutting more.

"I ought to ask you the same question though. I've been away only a wee bit compared to your eighteen year absence. Do you not miss New Callander?"

"Miss my birthplace?" She nearly cut her finger. "'Tis not my home anymore." She shrugged off his question. "After my parents and brother died, I no longer had any family left there. My closest relative lived here, so that's where they sent me."

"No flesh and blood family perhaps, but, Fiona, trust me, you still have friends and *family* there." A mist veiled her eyes and she whacked at the meat harder. "How is it that you never sent word to any of us after you left?"

He leaned his elbows on the table, and watched her rip the meat from the bones, or perhaps he studied her face. She knew not, because she didn't dare look at him—she'd unravel if she did.

"We were a close community, Fiona. We still are." He folded his hands on the table. "Everyone of us felt the loss of your family to Yellow Fever."

She stole a look at his face. His features were intent on her. "Do you suppose I wished to leave?" She tossed the last piece of meat into the bowl. "I didn't exactly travel here full of enthusiasm and wonder at my new life." With more force than necessary, she scraped her work surface to clear all the scraps into a pail for her pig to consume later. "Sure, I was fortunate I had an aunt here who loved me. But I missed my family terribly, and everything and everyone I had left behind. 'Twas never my wish to leave. And when my aunt married, I feared I might be in the way and they'd ship me someplace else. But, I was fortunate. My new uncle was a good man and he loved me as his daughter."

He rose to help her dump some potatoes onto the table for chopping. "You ought to have written," his gentle words reached her ears as the last of the taters hit the wood.

"I attempted to." Her hand rummaged through the pile of vegetables. "But 'twas too painful. I'd progress as far as setting out the parchment, but then as soon as I dipped my quill, the memories flooded back and my tears ruined the pages. Eventually, I found it easier just to push the memories away."

A strong arm spread across her shoulders. "I'm sorry. We ought to have tried to find you. But besides knowing that you were sent to live with an English Loyalist relative, we knew not where exactly in Upper Canada you had been sent."

"Oh, Lachlan, you have nothing to apologize for. I ought to have been stronger. I ought to have a least been able to write one sentence."

"Don't chide yourself. You were young and had much to deal with."

She leaned into his chest, and let her lids fall shut as she soaked up his reassurance. "I so dearly missed home. But by the time I grew old enough to write I thought everyone would have forgotten me and I'd just be rendering myself a fool."

"Not possible." His breath wafted through her hair. But a rustle by the door forced her eyes open. She met his pained gaze and knew he had heard the noise, as well.

When he pulled away, it felt as if he had been ripped from her. Nevertheless, he was correct to act swiftly, they couldn't be caught in an embrace. She busied herself with the potatoes whilst he left the kitchen to investigate.

"The men have become exceedingly hungry and I've been sent to hurry the cook." A soldier spoke after Lachlan greeted him.

Deep and definitive, Lachlan's voice was devoid of the gentleness he had used only moments before when he had spoken to her. "Dinner shall commence in approximately one hour. However, you may inform the men it shall be well worth the wait. We shall be feasting on squirrel stew and biscuits."

The sound of the American soldier rubbing his hands together in anticipation reached her. "I shall tell the men."

Lachlan waited for the soldier to depart before he returned to the kitchen. "I don't believe he witnessed us together." She dipped her chin and continued to busy herself. "I do however think it best if I return to the others." He grabbed his musket from the wall. But instead of leaving, he stood—torn.

"Lachlan—" he gripped his musket and his knuckles turned white with the soft way she had spoken his name "—please take my skillet down from beside the hearth. I ought to have retrieved it before I started the fire. 'Tis not as if I'm unaware of how easy it is to catch my gown in those flames. So many women do die from such accidents."

He watched her words flow fast from her lips and it caused him to smile. He had affected her, just as she had him.

"Certainly." He swiftly reached to take the three-foot long handled skillet off the hook. "May I help with anything else before I depart?"

"Nay." She reached for the skillet's black handle and their fingers touched. His eyes sought and held hers. Momentarily, the world, with all its problems, disappeared around them. "Thank you."

"Fiona—" He took a step closer to her.

A wet nose pressed into his other hand and jerked his senses back. "Hello there, Scolty." He patted her dog before he fixed his hat more firmly on his head.

"Scolty, how did you manage to escape the barn?" She frowned at the trail of rope still attached to him. "You've no doubt come in here because you smelled food." She bent down and rubbed behind his ear before the dog turned to lick her hand.

He sucked in a breath. Her smile and laughter shone like a candle flame that chased away the darkness in an unlit room. He had seen so much death and suffering in this war that the simple innocence of a dog with its mistress shook him—at least that's what he convinced himself had unnerved him.

"I shall see you in an hour." He straightened, and felt his muscles tighten back into their regular military form.

She wiped her hands on her white apron. "Before you go—" she walked to one of the cupboards that flanked her hearth "—I have a biscuit left over from my supper last night." She pulled one out of a jar. "Perhaps you'd be so kind as to tie up my dog better than I." She smiled, but stopped when her fingers brushed his. "'Tis better for him out of doors. 'Tis overly hot for him in here. And I shan't wish him to encounter another soldier." She returned the jar to the cupboard.

He nodded, then flipped the biscuit in his hand. "Your dog may fancy me after this." He smelled the hard, almost white biscuit that she'd soon bake for his regiment's dinner. His mouth watered.

"He already adores you. You saw to that earlier." She ran her hand along the front of her bib-closing gown and shook it a bit to fan herself in this heat. The movement seared his attention. He gulped.

"Come, Scolty. This treat belongs to you." He held the biscuit in front of the dog's nose, then led him out of doors into the glaring sun and chose a tree the soldiers ought not to pass. The dog followed him. "You must thank Fiona for this." He gave him a piece of the biscuit whilst he tied him up. "She's still incredible, is she not?" He looked down at the dog's eager face. "I know you agree with me." He broke off another morsel.

"'Twould be only too easy to get attached to her once more." He stroked the dog's fur. "But, I have my work. A post I take seriously. I'm not planning to remain an officer forever. I intend to move up the ranks."

A breeze rustled through the trees and his gut clenched. He couldn't explain why, but whenever his thoughts veered in this direction he felt as if God disagreed with him.

God, if You are disagreeing with me, I shall need something more tangible than the wind. Moses received a burning bush.

The dog's impatient, wet nose sniffed his hand. "Sorry, Scolty.

Here." He broke another bit of the biscuit and held it for the dog as his eyes sailed across Fiona's land to her home.

Her modest house, with chimneys that rose from opposite sides of the roof, emanated sweetness. A splatter of windows made it appear lively and happy. But had he just described her house or her?

He shook his head. He couldn't stop thinking about her. And a smile spread over his lips before he caught hold of himself. It had always been exceedingly easy to dream about a life with her as his wife.

"Last piece, Scolty." He watched the dog take the food and offered him a pat before he stood with what had to be a final glance at her home until dinner. And yet, even though he knew he ought to command his feet to march away, something caught his eye and drew his attention back toward her home.

Who was that?

*L*achlan's eyes focused on a man who appeared overly confident in his right to enter Fiona's home. A snake squeezed his heart when he realized he had only asked her if she had a husband, he had never inquired as to whether she had a beau.

His shoulders fell, until he noticed the man carried a bag. A medical bag? Was she ill? Uncertainty gripped his chest. "Come, Scolty." He untied the dog. "You must go in there."

Fiona quickly mixed the ingredients for biscuits. She blushed. Something about the way Lachlan had peered at her, and spoke to her, caused her to think he had intended to kiss her. She dropped the spoon and dashed from the kitchen. She needed to see him, even if 'twas just for one more moment.

Lachlan McAllister was here—on her homestead—after eighteen years—and she did indeed wish him to kiss her.

Her gaze sought him. But instead of his handsome form, a shadow darkened her doorway. Her hands clutched one another and she stiffened. *Why had the doctor come?*

"Fiona, my sweet." Edgar Blackstone's words turned her stomach. "Are you not well? My cousin informed me of your current situation."

In an attempt to block him from entering her home any farther, she crossed her arms and stood firm. "As you can see, I'm fine. I'm sorry Mrs. Johnson troubled you. There was no need to inconvenience yourself with a visit. A busy man, such as yourself, most certainly has plenty to do."

She stepped toward the door. Her stern composure a clear sign that he ought to yield and follow her hint to leave.

He removed his black beaver-felt top hat. "Nonsense." He passed her.

She closed her gaping mouth and dragged her feet into the kitchen. He leaned over the simmering black iron pot. His nostrils expanded as he sucked in the aroma. "Even though I carry the burden of being the best doctor in Upper Canada, you remain my first concern."

Me? She snickered to herself and spooned biscuit batter onto the skillet. *You shan't fool me. I know 'tis my land that concerns you.* She pursed her lips to keep her sentiments from escaping.

"Those are sure to please." He pointed at her biscuits, before he tapped his thin finger on his lips. If he had attempted to incite an invitation to dine, he best look elsewhere. She set the skillet over the open flames in the hearth.

After a moment of utter silence, the doctor drifted toward her. "Fiona, I've come to inform you of what's being said about you in town. All the inns, taverns, stores, and even the distilleries are flooded with the news of you, a single woman, alone with all these American soldiers."

She kept her eyes on the biscuits and stayed crouched down to distance herself from him. "You visited all those places, yourself, just this past morning?"

"Well." He coughed. "Let me simply proffer that all the good people of this town are convinced these American men have either taken advantage of you, and ruined you, or you're profiting from their business."

She gasped and jumped to her feet. "Is that so? Why then have none of the *good people of this town* come to help me themselves?"

"Alas, they've sent me." He smirked. "Now, I'm sure you're not profiting by having these American soldiers here, and that's why I'd never accuse you of any such wrong doing. But 'tis the talk of the town and I only know of one way to silence such prattle—" he grabbed her fingers and rammed them against his mouth "—marry me."

She wrenched her hand away. She didn't wish him anywhere near her, let alone kissing her. She strode past him to the table.

He followed her. "Fiona, our nuptials ought to quiet everyone for good."

"Thank you for your offer, Doctor. But—I—" she attempted to form words that ought not offend him, because nothing good would come from making either him, or his cousin, Mrs. Johnson, her enemy.

"I realize I've asked you previously, but 'twas in jest then, you must see the necessity of it now. You need me, Fiona." He clenched his teeth when she didn't respond. "I understand. You're much too virtuous of a woman to reply directly, so I shall part with you for now and allow you to pray upon it. But I shall return later this afternoon for your answer." He laid his hands on her shoulders, and if that didn't send bile burning up her throat, his warm breath in her ear did. "Please, marry me. We'd augment each other's lives exceedingly well."

She flew away from his touch when her dog's growl erupted into the house. "Scolty." She took hold of her dog by the collar. "Enough. Edgar was just leaving." She glared at the doctor. But he didn't seem to notice as he painstakingly put his top hat back on.

"I'm uncertain of the particulars surrounding what shall become of your dog once we marry, but we shall leave that for the future." He flashed his teeth at her.

A shiver ran along her spine. She clenched her jaw and refused to argue. His threat didn't matter. She'd never agree to marry him and nothing would ever cause her to.

Lachlan crept away from Fiona's kitchen door. He had overheard the last part of her conversation with that British man and that was enough.

How dare the man say, *"I'm uncertain of the particulars surrounding what shall become of your dog once we marry."* What did he plan to do to her dog? He glared as the man stalked to his horse unaware of him hiding in the shadows.

His chest grew tighter. How could Fiona consider marrying a man who'd alluded to banishing, or worse, exterminating, her dog?

God, it might be unchristian of me to dislike that man, but 'tis not simply because he wishes to wed Fiona—something is amiss here and I do not trust him.

The British man mounted his horse, and as soon as it trotted away, he reentered Fiona's home. Stopping just within the doorway, he watched her cook over the hearth. "Scolty," he called.

"Oh," she screeched. "You scared me."

"I apologize." He held his open palms up as he neared her. "'Twas not my intention to startle you."

"'Tis fine." She took a deep breath with her hand still pressed firmly over her heart.

"I came for Scolty." He took hold of the dog's rope. "But before I go, I couldn't help but see a man leave here scarcely a minute ago." She tensed and a frown settled on her face. "Is he a doctor? Are you ill?"

She shook her head, which relieved him immensely. "Doctor Edgar Blackstone was merely visiting. He's my neighbor."

"Oh." He took a deep, bewildered breath. Why hadn't she told him she was betrothed to the man? "I shall tie up Scolty." He grabbed a biscuit off the table and hurried out.

Leading the dog back to the tree, he couldn't help but mutter, "Even if she refuses to tell me she's betrothed, I cannot ignore what I overheard. I just hope for her sake that this doctor is a better man than

I believe him to be, because she deserves to be happy."

*   *   *

Wearily, Fiona fell into her sofa. Serving dinner had exhausted her. However, she still possessed a multitude of chores that needed tending to before she cooked supper. How many more days of this could she endure?

Plenty! She yelled at herself. Because that meant Lachlan shall remain here—safe. She simply needed a moment to rest. She closed her eyes and sank further into the cushions.

"Fiona?" she heard her name and her eyes fluttered open. "I'm sorry, did I wake you?"

"Aye." She stood so quickly her head felt light and Lachlan took her elbow. "But I'm thankful you did. I didn't intend to fall asleep."

"You overworked yourself." He moved in closer to her. "'Tis still early enough in the afternoon, please sit a moment longer. I saved you some biscuits." He held out a handkerchief laden with them. "I don't believe I saw you partake at dinner."

Stunned, she looked at what he had unwrapped. He had noticed she hadn't eaten and cared enough to save her some food. Her heart expanded. "Lachlan, these are your biscuits. You need to eat them. You need your strength." She pushed them back toward him.

However, he set them down on the tea table. "Eat them. I guarantee you I cannot." He patted his stomach. "Your stew filled me. And 'twas delicious, by the way."

"Thank you." She smiled before she took a biscuit and walked past him to avoid allowing him see her eyes well.

"I shall fetch more water. In this heat, I'm certain you must be in need of some."

"'Tis most thoughtful of you, thank you." She held in her tears as his footsteps faded. Aye, beyond a doubt, she cherished him here.

If Edgar loved Fiona, then why had he not stayed to tend to her?

Lachlan turned the handle to raise the bucket out of the well. The man was a doctor, he conceded, perhaps he had a patient that direly needed attention, because anything less, would never have been enough to pull Lachlan away.

"You're dripping wet again." Fiona chuckled, as he brought her a glass of water.

"This heat is relentless." He smiled.

She paused before she drank. "Shall you not drink?"

With a smirk, he looked himself over. "Believe me, I drank even more water than I poured over myself."

She laughed and then emptied her glass. "I had better make sure my animals have sufficient water."

"May I join you?"

"You needed bother. I can manage. I'm used to performing such work." She set the glass down. "'Tis part of my daily routine."

"I'm certain you work relentlessly to keep this homestead on your own, but we've added to your burden and I cannot stand to see you strain yourself more."

"You must have other things that need doing though. Or if not, some rest to catch up on?"

He searched her face, uncertain as to whether she was merely being polite, or if she truly did not wish him nearby. "I have nothing more pressing to do. The men are at the Niagara River fishing and I volunteered to stay behind lest orders come down from the higher ranks. So please, accept my help, as one old friend to another."

"*As one old friend to another?*" Her hazel eyes held his. "I'm uncertain about the term *old*, but the *friend* portion of your offer is acceptable." With a dip of his chin he smiled, then followed her to the barn with Scolty in tow.

"That was the final one," Fiona said, as Lachlan watched her animals leave the barn for the pasture before they headed to the stable.

"He's beautiful." He ran his hand over her Quarter Horse's flank.

"Thank you." She patted his muzzle and cooed at the brown horse.

"What did you name him?"

"I'd rather not say." She nestled her forehead against the horse's soft hair.

"Fiona, we've known each other since we were bairns. You cannot possibly feel bashful."

She stalled, then responded, "Forgive me, but 'tis a lass's name."

He couldn't halt his laughter. "Did you not know it to be a male before you named him?"

"Aye." She shook her head wryly. "I named him for what he signifies to me."

"And what pray tell is that?"

"Hope." She let out a breath. "Because I'm planning on procuring him a mate and breeding them."

His eyebrows shot up. An enormous dream to accomplish alone. But then he remembered her doctor. He'd help her. "You best keep him out of sight."

"Aye, I cannot lose him. Please, Lachlan, don't allow your men to seize him."

"I shall do my best." He dipped his chin, wishing instead of a mere attempt he'd been able to issue a guarantee. "I remember you always enjoyed to ride, and every spare moment you found you'd spend at our friend, Cole Munro's grandparent's ranch."

The brown and green of her eyes swirled into the past. "I learned everything I know about horses from Cait and Finnean. I only hope that one day I shall be able to live as they did, with horses paying my livelihood. Do the Munros still own their horse farm?"

He nodded. But he failed to understand—if she married the doctor, surely he ought to be able to support them. He opened his mouth, then shut it tight. She knew not that he'd overheard of her betrothal. "I hope God blesses you in your life, Fiona."

"Thank you. I hope the same for you." She glanced at him. "God knows I've been laboring hard to purchase that mare. Since my aunt and uncle died a few years back, I've been running this homestead whilst keeping the store open."

"I cannot fathom when you find time to sleep." He gave her horse a pat. "When do you anticipate being able to acquire a mare?"

"I believe I'm extremely close." She stepped out of her horse's stall.

"May I help to speed the process along?"

"Thank you. But, nay. You've already been an enormous help. I cannot accept any more of your kindness."

He shrugged. "If you ever need anything though, please ask."

Her eyes met his, and she gave him a quick nod, before she led them out of the stable.

"This heat is suffocating." He chose the most shaded path back to her house. "I propose we fetch some water for ourselves."

A smile lit her face. "As long as I'm allowed to drink it, instead of wear it, I agree with your wonderful suggestion."

"I promise I shan't wet you." He laughed. The doctor was a most fortunate man. "You first." He held the ladle out for her to drink from the well's bucket.

"Thank you." She handed it back and took hold of the bucket while he drank.

"That certainly felt good." He wiped his mouth.

"Not as good as this shall feel." She swung the bucket toward him and the contents sailed through the air, landing with a heavy splash.

"Fiona!" He shook the water off.

She dropped the bucket and retreated. "Remember your promise," she chuckled. "You vowed not to wet me."

"That I did." Momentum propelled him toward her. "And I always keep my promises. But as an officer, I believe a retaliation is in order." Her eyes grew large. "I do remember a certain young lass to be extremely ticklish."

"You shan't." She pushed her hands out toward him to create a shield. "We're adults now, we must behave as such."

"You're correct. As an adult I shall be much more fair," he smirked. "I shall count to three." She gasped, then lifted her skirts, turned and ran toward her home. "One, two, three," he counted in quick succession, then raced after her.

Grabbing her waist, he tickled her. She turned to protest. Her face mere inches from his as her back bumped against the wall. Their laughter ceased.

His hands stilled on her waist. Hers rested against his chest. Their eyes beheld each other. He studied every brown and green fleck, until she bit her lip.

He brushed a strand of her light brown hair away from her face and her lips parted as she inhaled.

The desire to kiss her stormed through him. And yet he pushed himself back from the wall. She wasn't his to kiss. She belonged to the doctor.

Fiona's chest heaved as she stared at Lachlan's broad back. She knew exactly what that look in his eyes had meant. But why had he not kissed her?

She took a step toward him. She wished to say something, yet she was completely unable to think of anything.

But she must try. She shan't
allow this to ruin the friendship they
had rekindled. "Lachlan—" She
swallowed hard as he turned and his
brown orbs pierced hers. She saw
regret in his depths. Although she
didn't know if 'twas from almost
kissing her, or for not kissing her.

"Fiona—" His utterance sounded
as unsure as hers had been. And then
she saw it—the future they ought to
have enjoyed if her family had never
died of Yellow Fever and she hadn't
been sent away. The age difference she
had thought such a monumental obstacle
back then would have vanished as they
grew older together. She would have
come to love him, just as she was
beginning to now. "I'm sorry I tickled
you."

"I'm sorry I wet you."

They stood in silence.

"Lachlan—" her brows knotted
together "—do you smell that?"

His gaze darted around her
homestead. "It smells as if something
is burning."

*T*error seized Fiona. She looked to her home, but no smoke came from it. And none came from her store either. However, she couldn't see her barn or the stable from where they stood.

"Lachlan, we must untie Scolty

and then see to my animals." He didn't answer. He just took her hand and they ran.

She stumbled and his hand gripped hers tighter. She felt the blood drain from her head and knew she must have blanched by the look of concern on his face as he untied her dog. Her stomach revolted, but she had to push the horrible memories out of her mind. Her animals needed her.

Nearing the barn and stable, she couldn't see any smoke there either. "What if the woods surrounding my home are aflame?" Her eyes searched them. "The animals still out in the pasture may be in danger."

Again he took her hand and they raced on. "I see the smoke." He pointed toward the Niagara River. "It must be coming from the soldiers."

Her heart began to slow to a canter. The fire burnt under control. "But what induced them to start a fire in the middle of the afternoon, especially in this heat?" He shrugged. "Did they help themselves to my firewood?"

"Do you not store your wood by the house?" She nodded. "Then, I doubt they journeyed thus far to retrieve it. Fiona, I wish to check on something, do you wish to come with me?" She nodded.

"What's the matter, Lachlan?" The look on his face lay contrary to her relief. "I don't mind the men cutting down a couple of my trees. In fact, I might come to appreciate them clearing a bit more land."

"I doubt the men cut down any of your trees."

"Then how have they built such a large fire? 'Tis not possible for them to have collected that many pinecones and twigs. And anyway, it shan't have produced that much smoke or smelled as such." She inhaled deeply, but she couldn't ascertain what they had burnt to exact such an odor.

Then she noticed the destruction. Her animal enclosure now missed vast sections of its wood fence. "The men tore this down to build their fire?" She wiggled a lone fence post.

"I'm sorry." He surveyed the damage.

"'Tis not your fault. None of this is. And I cannot worry about it now anyway, because I must find my animals. If they wander too far, I shall never retrieve them, and come nightfall, they shall fall prey to wolves or wildcats."

He increased his pace. "There's a goose." He ran and fought to secure hold of it. She led them back to the barn and opened the door. "Lachlan—" she shut the animal in "—your hands are cut." She reached for them.

But he pulled away. "We must hurry. Your chickens are heading down to the river, but they're moving slow enough that we ought to be able to round them up before they reach it."

She ran alongside him. Once they neared her chickens she released her dog and commanded him to herd the fowl toward the barn. Lachlan grabbed several birds that had meandered away. She winced each time a chicken clawed at him and drew more blood. He looked as if he had been in battle.

"All the chickens are safe." She closed the barn door. "That leaves the rooster, the cows, and my pig, Big

Bonnie." She mopped her forehead with her handkerchief. "The rooster ought to be able to find his own way home, and the cows shall wander back in search of their supper later. Hence, the only animal left to find is my pig. But before we search for her, I shan't accept any arguements, you must allow me to wash and bandage your hands."

"Aye, Ma'am." He stood as tall and straight as if she were his colonel.

She grimaced. "I'm sorry if I sounded harsh, but I cannot permit you to go about wounded." They walked back to her house with Scolty.

"I'm sorry my men's fire scared you."

She shrugged. "Again, 'tis not your fault. This homestead is all I have and I cannot imagine my life if I lost it."

He looked down at her dog, whose tongue wagged from overexertion. "But you appeared terrified, more so than when we invaded your home?"

She wrung her hands. "My aunt and uncle died in an attempt to save animals in a fire at a neighbor's barn." He stopped and his eyes bored into hers. "The smoke brought back the memory of that day. I can still hear their screams, feel the arms that clung to me to hold me in place." She shuddered. "I shall never forget that roof caving in on them."

He hugged her tight. "I'm sorry."

"So am I," she whispered into his chest. "I couldn't save them." With an arm still around her, he led her into the house. "You ought not to be comforting me though. I'm supposed to be mending your hands." She forced a smile and moved away from him toward the stairs. "Please, sit in the kitchen. I shall return in a moment."

The tears she had fought to keep inside stormed out in a relentless flood the moment she turned her back to him.

In her bedroom, she composed herself. *God, I know I've experienced tragedy in my life, but I still thank You for all my blessings. And one of them is sitting in my kitchen.*

She picked up her washbasin and pitcher, then descended the stairs. He sat straddled over the bench in front of her kitchen table. His vivid eyes met hers. He must have been thinking of her as he sat awaiting her return.

After placing the pitcher and washbasin on the table, she retrieved the kettle. He didn't speak, but his eyes followed her.

She poured the water, procured some cloths, and swallowed when she saw him still regarding her. Submerging the material into the warm water, she squeezed out the excess. The dripping water was the only noise in the house.

She sat sideways in front of him. Without a look to his face she took his right hand. She shifted in her seat toward him. He felt warm as she dabbed at his cuts.

With his eyes still upon her, her heart beat fitfully, but she pushed on with her task. When she was satisfied that she had cleansed his right hand, she took a different cloth and patted his skin dry.

Reaching for his left hand, she dared a glance at his face and found his brown depths still intent upon her. She bit her lower lip and dropped her gaze back down to his hand as she cleaned it.

By the time she finished drying that hand, she felt as if the room held no more air.

"Thank you." He sprang from her bench. The legs wobbled and clattered against her wood floor.

"Wait." She rose from the jostling. "I still need to bandage them."

"They're fine. Scabs shall form soon enough." He examined them as he backed away. "You performed the task with greater skill than our surgeon at Fort George. I've seen men die from infections setting in on cuts little worse than this." He blew on his hands. "I think we ought to find your pig." He darted for the door.

"Wait for me. I wish to come."

"I shall wait out of doors." He left the kitchen.

She grabbed hold of a chair and stared after him as she blew out a breath. Had he been as touched by their encounter as she had been?

She threw the dirty water out the back door, washed the bowl, and set the cloths to soak before she went in search of him.

She found him sitting with his back against a maple tree. He wasn't wearing his hat and his thick brown hair waved slightly in the—almost imperceptible—breeze. His long white overalls covered strong legs that stuck out before him, with one black gaiter crossed over the other. His hands lay healing on his lap and his eyes were closed. If he napped, she shan't wake him.

She sighed, noticing his white vest, and belt, and how much the blue of his coat suited him. What a man he had grown into. And yet, her heart ached for the Lachlan she had known. The impetuous lad, whom she thought used to love her when they were young. The one who would have already declared his marriage proposal—if he still loved her.

She backed away, if only he did still love her. She stepped on a twig. It snapped and his eyes flew open. "Sorry." She covered her mouth.

He was upright before she could retreat any farther. "Are you ready to search for your pig?" She nodded, as he stretched.

Her mouth opened to tell him she could go alone, but she clamped it shut. He would reject that suggestion. And her chest squeezed with the thought of how protective he behaved toward her.

They set off. The smoke continued to billow in the sky. And she still couldn't fathom what else the soldiers had burned to produce that smell. However, she wasn't about to question Lachlan. She knew he couldn't divulge any information about his regiment.

"Do you see her?" She questioned him when he stopped to stare into the distance.

"Nay, but I think I see my fellow officer approaching, and I must speak with him."

"I shall continue to search for Big Bonnie."

He glanced at her. "Why do you call her that? I've never known anyone to name a pig. Do you have names for all your chickens, as well?" He chuckled, as he held up his scabbed hands. "Because if you don't, might I suggest, Scratchy, Clawer, Spiteful and Mean-Spirited."

She laughed. "I know people consume pigs, and I eat pork as well, but not Big Bonnie. I consider her my pet. My uncle presented her to me whilst she was a tiny piglet and she worked her way into my heart. Now she's the only living reminder of my aunt and uncle."

He nodded. "We must find her soon then. This conversation ought not take long." He jogged away.

She called for her pig. But not a single snort came, and no hoof prints presented themselves, nor any other markings to show her pig had even walked out of the barn.

"Fiona," Lachlan's voice interrupted her thoughts a while later. His face appeared pinched. Something had happened. Her feet froze to the ground. He was to leave. Another battle was about to be waged.

"Pray tell, what news have you?" She held a hand to her chest. "What is to come?"

"I shall see you home." Lachlan looked past Fiona into the woods behind her.

She nodded and followed him. "It has become late," she conceded with narrowed eyes as she watched him. "I certainly ought to have begun supper by now."

He rubbed the back of his neck and kept his head down as they walked. She in turn wrung her hands with the thought of what troubled him.

"I shall continue to search for Big Bonnie after supper. There shall still be enough daylight."

He didn't respond, not even a grunt to signify that he had heard her.

She stopped. "Lachlan, this silence worries me. You must tell me what has happened. What troubles you?" She laid a hand on his arm. "Please, I'm your friend. I shall take anything you share with me to my grave. Forget this war. Speak to me."

Her pleas met with the most sorrowful eyes. "I'm sorry, but you needn't cook supper tonight."

She smiled. "See now," she joked, in an attempt to ease whatever afflicted him. "That's not such bad news. I didn't particularly relish cooking dinner for everyone earlier." He rubbed his musket. Sadness gripped her tighter than a noose around her neck. "Are you to depart?"

He laid his arm across her shoulder and his touch only made the thought of never seeing him again that much worse. "You shall wish us all gone once you learn the truth," he murmured.

"I beg your pardon?" Her eyebrows pulled together. "What truth do you refer to?"

He exhaled. "After the men tore down your fence, they saw what they thought was a wild boar, so they caught her, and—"

"Nay." She shook her head. "Don't finish that sentence." She squirmed away from his embrace. "Do not say the words." Tears burst from her eyes. The air was too heavy and she gasped for breath. Her pig, her pet, her Big Bonnie was gone. Sobs tore through her chest.

Would God leave her anything to love? She chastised herself the moment the thought entered her mind. *God forgive me. But I never supposed that she would die that way.*

More tears came and she didn't
fight Lachlan when he put his arms
around her. She burrowed into his blue
coat, feeling his hand weave through
her hair. One by one she was losing
everyone and everything she loved. How
long until she would lose this
homestead altogether and her dream of
breeding horses along with it?

And, Lachlan, too, would be a
mere memory soon enough. She wrapped
her arms around him and squeezed him
close. She hadn't hugged anyone since
her aunt and uncle's last day on
earth.

"I'm sorry, Fiona," his soothing
voice engulfed her, as he pressed her
head gently into him. "I'm so sorry."

Lachlan caressed Fiona's hair. It
was soft, like he had imagined it
would be and it smelled of lavender.
Holding her tightly to him, he let her
cry.

His heart hurt with each sob she
spilled into his chest. His men had
taken away her pet, and along with
that, they had reopened a devastating

wound. What he wouldn't do to change that.

He strengthened his embrace and felt her slender arms wrap around him with such force that her movement caused him to stop breathing. She was hugging him back, holding him firm. He hadn't had a woman in his arms like this before. He had never held anyone as close to his heart as he had held her. Images of a life with her swam through his mind.

But she was merely grieving, he censured himself, she didn't possess any amorous feelings for him. She was betrothed to that doctor.

He kissed her head and let his lips linger before he pulled away. "I'm sorry, but I see my fellow officer approaching once more." She wiped at her tear-streaked face, but kept her head down, as if embarrassed. "Please take yourself indoors. I shall go to meet him so he shan't journey this far."

She nodded and took a step away from him before she spun around and grasped his hand. "Thank you." He squeezed her hand back and then she reached up on tiptoe and kissed his cheek. His eyes remained glued to her as she went into her house. She had definitely just taken a piece of his heart with her.

"Lachlan," his other regimental officer addressed him, after he had marched out a considerable distance to greet him. "I've just heard news."

He dipped his chin. He knew they were only staying here a day at most, but 'twas still difficult to hear the orders. "The Colonel confirmed that we shall be marching to attack the outpost at DeCou's house near Beaver Dams at daybreak. He's certain this surprise attack shall garner us a victory over the British."

He nodded. He knew the realities of such a plan—lives would be lost tomorrow.

*   *   *

Fiona swatted a fly as she busied herself in the kitchen. She couldn't spend any more time weeping. She must hurry and cook something for her supper, because the men would come to sleep soon and she had no desire to be present when they returned.

Mixing oats into boiling water, her hand strangled the wooden spoon knowing she must cook breakfast for the men who had slaughtered her pet.

She closed her eyes and an image of her aunt and uncle flashed before her. She knew precisely what they would've said if they had been here. *At least you hadn't been hurt or killed.* Aye, she knew she had been fortunate to have Lachlan to mind her. "Thank you, God, for sending him to me," she spoke aloud.

"Those are precisely the words every man takes pleasure in hearing."

She spun on her heel and the bowl she had held clattered to the floor. "I didn't hear you knock, Edgar." She stooped to pick up the wooden vessel.

"I apologize, but I do remember telling you I'd return later in the day for your answer. You ought to have been expecting me."

She wiped her hands on a towel. *Dear God, help me speak my words properly.* "I remember." She folded the towel and laid it upon the table

before she stirred her oatmeal. "Have
you eaten supper?" she stalled.

"I have, but I shall be remiss if
I don't join you."

"Please, sit then." She ladled
oatmeal into a bowl and placed it
before him. "Do you fancy molasses?"

"I shan't stomach this without
it." She stopped herself from wincing
and served him politely. However, she
did set the dark jar down with a thud,
before she fixed herself a bowl.
"I apologize I have not more to offer
you, but I scarcely found time to cook
to-day."

"Oh?" His dark eyebrows shot up
with accusation. "Pray tell, why?"

Her hands tightened into fists,
but she took a deep breath and calmed
herself. "Some of my animals became
loose and I spent the afternoon
recapturing them."

She moved oatmeal around with her
spoon. Not much remained in the pot,
and if for any reason Edgar wished for
more, she must save enough for Lachlan
lest he be hungry.

"That explains your rosy
complexion," he sneered.

She ignored him, knowing full well his words were not a compliment. "Do you fancy some tea?" She crossed the room to retrieve two cups.

"I did wonder when you'd offer."

She closed her eyes and took another deep breath. There was nary a doubt in her mind that he only wished to marry her for her land. Because forget about him loving her, he didn't even convey the impression that he liked her. Hence, 'twas inconceivable that she'd spend her life under his rule. Another minute in his presence was more than she could bear.

"Shall I serve you more oatmeal?" She poured the tea, as he scraped the remnants of molasses from his bowl.

"If you must."

She bit her tongue. Did he actually believe he did her a kindness by consuming her food? She set her untouched bowl out of sight and ladled the remnants of the pot into his bowl.

"And please don't neglect to pour molasses on top."

She fought to stretch her lips in a pleasant manner. "I shan't ever dream of insulting you with such a transgression." She sat down in the wooden chair opposite him.

"It pleases me to hear that you care, and it bodes well for the reason I'm here." He sat back when he had finished, and pushed his empty vessel forward, as if it now repulsed him. "You've remained alone in this house all day with American gentlemen—"

"I fail to see any *gentlemen* here now," she interrupted, with a smile to herself at the word he had failed to understand. "Nor were there any *gentlemen* here whenst you visited earlier."

Was that the reason he hadn't knocked? Had he hoped to catch her with a man?

"Permit me to reword my speech in terms more befitting for *you* to understand." He flashed his teeth. "You've been alone on this *homestead* all day with American soldiers. The town is already afire with speculation of your immoral conduct, and after you spend the night here unchaperoned, not even I shall be able to squash the rumors that shall arise."

"As I've previously expressed, I shall sleep, *by myself*, in my store." She failed to banish the hostility from her voice.

"That may well happen, but the damage to your reputation has already occurred. You need me to resolve this on your behalf." What she needed was for him to leave. "But the only way I know to accomplish that, is if you accept my proposal of marriage. As my betrothed, you shall be above any disparaging remarks. Women shall revere you. It shall elevate your standing in the community."

She folded her hands together and took yet another deep breath. "I appreciate your offer, but I trust that the people of Queenston shan't cast stones without evidence. They ought to believe what I tell them. 'Tis the truth—nothing untoward has happened, or shall happen, to compromise my good name." She flashed him a faint smile. "So as you see, I need not marry you. But again, I thank you for your concern and your offer to help."

His nostrils flared. "Seeing as you're either foolishly naive or unreasonably stubborn, I must press the issue." He leaned forward in his chair. "I'm sorry to have the displeasure of disagreeing with you, but I assure you, your reputation has already been tarnished." He ran a hand through his black hair, which darkened the look of frustration on his face. "And you shall endure a difficult life here if you choose not to marry me."

Had he just threatened her? "I apologize." Her chair screeched along the floor as she stood. "But even if we conversed until the wee hours of morning, I don't believe we shall ever reach an agreement."

"If you shan't listen to reason, at least have enough sense to realize that by tarnishing your name you indeed soil your late aunt and uncle's names, and hence by association, mine." He rose to his full height. "Your uncle was my uncle long before he ever married your aunt."

"I am fully aware of that fact. But what we have yet to establish is whether your marriage proposal is

genuinely due to your concern for me
or if there is another reason you
insist upon it."

Silence descended upon them.

"This marriage shall benefit us
both." He pushed in his chair.

She smirked. "You've proclaimed
rather clearly how this marriage shall
benefit me, but you have yet to
explain how you shall benefit."

His fingers threatened to snap
the chair they menaced. "Why must you
persist in this foolish attempt to
thwart me?" His hands flew in the air.
"Do you not care that everyone in town
shall look down upon you? We can
settle on some sort of beneficial
arrangement pertaining to marriage."

She remained behind her chair.
Thankful that the table separated
them. "I fail to comprehend how a
marriage functions properly without
love."

"You had not the good fortune of
meeting my parents or you'd have
witnessed their flawless
exemplification of how to coincide
under such an agreement. Every day
they toiled in an effort to live their

lives for God. They bothered not with such silly amorous nonsense. Their marriage was decided for them and they rose to the task."

"I do apologize, but I could never view matrimony as a *task* to be endured. Truly, I am sorry."

He stomped toward her. She stepped back and bumped into the cupboard behind her. Without anywhere to move, she stilled as he towered over her.

"Not as sorry as you shall be. There are rumors circulating about you. Marrying me shall be to your benefit." He worked his jaw. "But I shall humble myself once more to ask—" he rested his hand beside her neck on the cupboard, as he bent down so his face was less than a few inches from hers "—shall you agree to become my wife?"

Her whole body quivered, but she shook her head. "I'm sorry. I cannot marry for any reason other than love. I hope one day you shall come to understand my reasoning."

"I shall never understand such sentimental rubbish." Her eyes winced shut as his fist smashed into the cupboard beside her head. "Precisely as I shall never understand the reason my uncle bestowed this land to you instead of me." He pointed to his chest. "I'm his nephew."

Her heart thumped hard as he stalked out of her kitchen. She continued to shake—even after he slammed her entrance door shut.

Lachlan's steps halted in the shadow of a maple tree, as a dark-haired man left Fiona's home. It must be the doctor, the man who rightfully ought to be there to console her after her pet's tragic death.

He had no need to go to her now.

Except, he wished to see her one last time.

When the doctor rode away, he approached her house. 'Twas the first time he had come upon her door shut. And in to-day's heat, he knew not how she had survived the temperature withindoors.

He tapped on the wooden barrier.

"Who's there?" she called.

"'Tis I, Lachlan." The lock clicked and she opened the door with red eyes. Guilt punched him in the stomach. She must have cried this entire time.

"I just finished gathering a few final items before I spend the night in my store." Her hands shook. Why hadn't the doctor been able to calm her? "I knew not for certain if you had eaten, so I saved you some oatmeal." She offered him a bowl.

"Thank you. That was most considerate of you. It shall be the perfect addition to the white fish and black bass I ate."

Her eyes held his for a moment, before she produced the quickest smile. He stirred the grainy porridge, glad to know she understood he hadn't consumed her pig.

"Oh, I forgot, before we leave, do you wish for me to pour molasses on that?"

He looked down at the generous serving of oatmeal. "Nay. It appears delicious just as is." She stared at him again. This time however he knew not why. But he didn't ask, as she hastily ventured out of doors.

"I feel rather odd leaving my house for the night." She glanced behind her.

"I feel horrible asking you leave your home. But you mustn't fret, the men who come tonight shan't ruin it. They shall only sleep here." She gave him a curt nod.

When they reached her store, she unlocked the door and set her things upon the table. He sauntered over to sit on the stoop and eat his oatmeal.

"Thank you for the warm treat," he said once she sat beside him. She smiled, then turned her attention to the setting sun as he finished eating.

When he laid his spoon to rest, he put the bowl down beside him and they sat in quietude for a while.

"I know my regiment caused you an abundance of trouble to-day, but I hope you shan't begrudge my delight in having found you."

"I am most glad of that, as well." Her voice was soft and low.

"If I reach home—"

Her head jerked sideways and her eyes implored him. "Please, you mustn't say *if*."

He dipped his chin. "*When* I reach home, everyone shall be pleased to know you're doing well for yourself up here." The scoff that escaped her lips caught him off guard. "Fiona?" He watched emotions flutter across her features. "You are fine, are you not?"

She faced him. "Please, you mustn't concern yourself with worrisome thoughts of me. I've been taking care of myself for years."

He dipped his chin to appease her, but worry still gnawed at him. "After this war ends, if you ever find yourself in need of help, I hope you shan't hesitate to write to me."

"Thank you." She ran a finger through her light brown hair, then twisted a strand before she let the curl fall along her neck.

"Actually, Fiona, I must retract my last words." She looked at him, her hazel eyes full of questions. "What I ought to have said, is that after this war ends, I hope you shall write, whether or not you need help. I wish

to remain in communication with
you—hear about your exploits, read
that you're happy." He swallowed.
'Twould hurt to have her confirm that
she had married the doctor, had a
large brood of beautiful children, and
was blissfully content.

She wiped at her eyes. "I shall
delight in that, as well."

"What particular part are you
most fond of?" He couldn't cope with a
tearful farewell. "Writing to me or
being happy?"

"Both." She grinned and leaned
over to knock her shoulder into him.

He smiled back. "I agree, why
limit ourselves with just one option?
But please, promise me you shall take
care of yourself."

"I do indeed always try. But I'm
not the officer in this war. 'Tis you
who ought to promise to be careful. I
shan't wish to write only to receive a
response that you've been killed." The
last word stuck in her throat and
their eyes met once more.

"Please keep me in your prayers
then." He took her hand and she
squeezed his fingers. She had stopped

shaking soon after she had sat down and now her hand felt warm and calm. "Do you remember all the times we sat out with your brother to watch the sunset?"

"Aye." She looked at the pink sky.

A nervous laugh escaped him. "I feel as if I must confess to not watching a single one." Her eyes grew as he kissed her hand. "I was completely and hopelessly in love with you back then." A smile slowly drew up her lips. "No matter what happens in this life, Fiona, please remember our time together as a pleasant memory."

She nodded and tears slid down her cheeks. He wiped one away and she dried the others before she pressed her lips into his cheek.

Moving closer to him, she laid her head on his arm. "Life may have differed greatly had I not been sent here to live."

He touched his lips to the top of her soft hair. Breathing her in, he placed his arm across her back and rested his head on hers. He would hold her like this for as long as she wished. But he knew the night sky would win. Time was not on his side.

*   *   *

A shriek shocked Fiona awake. Her heart pounded, even though 'twas her who had put the night into disquiet. 'Twas only a dream, she hugged herself. But in it, she had seen her parents and brother. They were back in their home. Everyone was happy. Then they started to vanish. One by one. Until only she had been left. She had shouted at them to come back, but they never returned.

She hadn't dreamt about them in ages. However, with Lachlan here, she ought to have expected a fretful night. She wrapped her shawl about her. 'Twould be fruitless to attempt to sleep again. She needed fresh air and a conversation with God.

But tonight she couldn't simply just walk out of doors. There may be American soldiers on patrol. She peered out her window. The night appeared clear and still.

She opened the door. Without the sun, the day's insufferable heat had retreated, and crisp air flooded her lungs as she stepped out. Crickets greeted her with their incessant songs, and the waning crescent moon barely lit her way to the outdoor chair.

The night was peaceful. Now if only her heart could remain so. She stopped. The chair before her wasn't empty. A man slumbered there. She inched closer. Could it be Lachlan? Her smile spread wide. He must have slept there to guard her.

She tiptoed back in her store and retrieved the quilt he had admired that morning. To ward off a chill, she laid the fabric over him. He didn't stir. He looked incredibly content, and she wished for nothing more than to stay and study his handsome features. But she knew she couldn't stay out there all night. Only a moment more, she promised herself. She didn't wish to wake him. He needed his sleep. "Sweet dreams, Lachlan," she whispered. "God bless, you."

"Fiona."

She froze.

But his eyes remained shut.

"Fiona," he mumbled in his sleep again.

She stared at him. What if he woke and saw her standing over him? She took a step back, then scampered within.

With the door closed behind her, her heart raced. He had dreamt of her. The smile on his face was unmistakable, and so was hers.

*   *   *

Fiona exited her store and glanced at the chair Lachlan had slept in the night before. Thinking of him sleeping there caused her to smile anew. *God, is it possible that he still harbors feelings for me?*

She picked up the quilt he had folded neatly and left in his place. Rubbing its softness against her cheek, she slowly inhaled his lingering scent. He was a good man. She remembered everything he had done for her yesterday, and an idea to treat him to a special meal settled in her mind.

Although, first she must cook breakfast for his regiment. She set about her morning tasks with gusto, eager to see him come for his meal.

But, he never came.

Had his duties as an officer kept him away, or had he sought to avoid her?

With slumped shoulders, she rode into town to purchase what she hoped ought to delight him. However, the ride provided her with an excessive amount of time to think, or, more to the point, to worry. She hadn't set eyes on her dog all morning either, and he never missed an opportunity to run alongside her horse. Her stomach knotted. She held a hand to it, perhaps Lachlan and Scolty were together.

She jumped down from her saddle. Now that she had arrived, she might as well obtain the mutton before she returned home to find them. Lachlan did love that meat. She grinned with the anticipation of surprizing him with it.

Hurrying to tie her horse in
front of the butcher's shop, she
glanced about. Her eyebrows pinched
together. *Most odd.* People moved away
from her. Women whispered and giggled
to each other. And as she stepped
toward the store, conversations
hushed.

With her head held high, she
walked on. God knew the rumors to be
false. However, when she heard a man
whistle and express a string of vulgar
words, worthy of a tavern, she put her
chin to her chest and hurried into the
shop.

Her heart thumped wildly. No one
had ever spoken to her that way
before, and she fought to hold back
tears. She was not one of *those* women.

She clasped her shaking hands
together. *Just purchase the mutton,
then run back to your horse, and he
shall race you home.* She created that
much of a plan. But how would she ever
resolve this calamity?

She inhaled a deep breath. *First,
purchase the mutton.* She reaffirmed
her plan as she took her place behind
two other women who waited in the line

at the counter that stretched across
the left side of the room. But before
she put her words into action, Mrs.
Johnson bustled toward her.

*T*he tight expression on Mrs. Johnson's face didn't surprise Fiona, not after she had rejected the doctor's proposal yesterday. Surely marrying Edgar couldn't be the only way to silence the gossips.

Anger surged through her. She was too close to obtaining a mare for her Quarter Horse to stop now. Nothing, or no one, would deter her from realizing her dream of breeding horses. She had been managing her homestead alone for years, and she shan't cower now. "Good morning, Mrs. Johnson."

"Do not *good morning* me lass." Mrs. Johnson stopped before her with a huff. "I simply cannot fathom why ye refused Edgar's proposal? He only had yer best interest at heart. Ye should hear all the vile, slanderous things being spoken about ye." Unfortunately, she had just heard more than enough. "My cousin—the kind and caring man that he is—only sought to help ye."

To keep her temper even, she squeezed her lips shut and glanced at some goods displayed on a shelf that began on her right and continued to the back of the store. Mrs. Johnson would only deny that Edgar wished to marry her for her land.

"I do hope ye come to yer senses and accept him." The matron's hands balled on her hips. "He's not too proud of a man to refuse a sensible woman who realizes her error and apologizes."

"I thank you for advising me on such matters, but I must apologize for not having the time to devote to thoughts of marriage to-day, I still have a homestead crowded with soldiers."

The woman laughed. "I do not know if I ought to pity ye, as Edgar has, or berate ye, because the American soldiers have all departed."

Her heart stopped. "Departed?"

"Aye." Mrs. Johnson shook her head. "Ye didn't notice the soldiers leave?"

"Nay." She had attempted to maintain her distance from the soldiers as she focused on her work, then she had come into town.

"They departed this morning. They were marching toward John and Catherine's house near Beaver Dams."

She glared at her. "How do you know this?"

Mrs. Johnson shuffled her feet impatiently on the wooden floor. "The Americans were deep in discussion at

Laura's house and she overheard their plans."

And now the entire town knew, as well, Fiona nearly scoffed. So that was why Mrs. Johnson had come into town to-day, more gossip needed to be spread.

"Seems those Americans planned a surprise attack on our British forces, but they're the ones who shall receive it." She nodded with smug satisfaction. "Laura set out a long while before they did to warn our men, and if she's able to outpace them, she shall warn our soldiers who shall be ready for those Americans, and hence, easily defeat them."

She grasped hold of the shelf. Her head spun and her stomach roiled. Lachlan was marching into a trap.

"Are ye not well?" Mrs. Johnson's words reached her ears, but she couldn't focus on them, she needed to return home.

This couldn't be happening. Mrs. Johnson must be mistaken. She must have received incorrect information. Lachlan couldn't be gone.

"Excuse me, but I must go." She released her grip on the shelf.

Utterly perplexed, Mrs. Johnson looked her over. "But ye never bought whatever 'tis ye travelled all the way into town for."

"I've chosen against purchasing it. Good day." She stalked out the door, and remembering how Lachlan had pinned looks on his soldiers, she imitated him as she scowled at the townspeople whilst she fled to her horse.

He couldn't be gone. He wouldn't have left without saying goodbye. She rode Hope home in a manner that befitted her race horse.

She didn't see any blue coats as they approached. But she still couldn't believe he had left. He must be here. He had to be safe.

She jumped down, and in her haste, stumbled to the ground before she ran into her house. Her eyes darted around wildly. The rooms were untidy—evidence the soldiers had been there—but otherwise, everything lay quiet.

She raced upstairs. Each room stood empty. She peered out every window, but she saw nothing but trees in every direction. Out of breath, she sunk into her wooden rocking chair and stared at her bare white walls. He was gone.

Please, God, take care of him. Tears welled in her eyes. If the British were waiting with their Native allies for the Americans, they'd surprise them, and the Americans may all be killed—including Lachlan.

Oh, Laura, what have you done? She fell onto the floor at the foot of her bed to pray. But before she even put her hands together, she realized what she must do. She must act just as Laura had at the Battle of Queenston Heights. Laura had found her husband and pulled him off the battlefield to safety.

She must find Lachlan.

Treason or not, she must warn him. She must save him before he was taken as a prisoner of war, or worse, scalped. She must reach him before 'twas too late. He couldn't die in this battle.

She stood, willing her legs to stop shaking. *God, please keep him alive.* She turned to leave, ready to ride out, but a folded piece of paper on top of her bureau halted her movement.

Guessing what lay written on the paper, and whom 'twas from, tears fell from her eyes. She wiped them away, determined to read the letter.

My Dearest Fiona,
This letter is written to say goodbye. We received official orders to set out late this morning. I apologize for not speaking to you directly regarding this matter, but I know you understand my military obligations.

Please know I shall treasure the time we shared together and I shall think upon it fondly.

Until we meet again, take care of yourself. I pray God shall help you fulfill your dreams.

You shall always remain in my thoughts and in my heart. And I sincerely do hope you shall write to me.

Yours,
Lachlan McAllister
P.S. Please release Scolty
from your barn. He had been
following me about all morning,
hence I locked him in there to
assure he'd be unable to follow
me into battle.

Tears streamed down her cheeks.
She clutched the letter to her chest.
God, help me. I must find him.

After setting Scolty free, she
ran to her horse and pulled herself up
into the saddle. "Scolty, go eat. You
cannot come with us now." The dog
didn't appear convinced. "Go. I shan't
allow you into the woods to be
attacked by wild animals." She
pointed, but the dog didn't pay her
any heed.

She ought to have left him in the
barn. He'd be safer in there, even in
this heat. But, when she calculated
the time needed to lock him up once
more, she resigned the matter.

"Fine, I grant you permission to
come. But please, if you understand
anything I'm saying, don't get hurt. I

shall have enough trouble keeping myself from getting shot or arrested."

They set off. She kept her eyes downward and looked for footprints, broken branches, or any other trail imprints to guide her. She also listened for musket shots and war cries, but she never saw or heard anything. As she neared Beaver Dams she feared the battle had already been waged. Nevertheless, she prayed it hadn't begun.

She couldn't save her parents and brother from dying of Yellow Fever, and she couldn't rescue her aunt and uncle from that barn fire, but God-willing, she would help Lachlan.

She pushed her horse faster and her dog followed along. "Come on, Hope. Only a wee bit farther."

She glanced down at her dog. But he no longer ran alongside her. She swung her head about, but couldn't see him anywhere.

Nay, not now. This was not the time for him to chase after a rabbit or some other creature. He couldn't become lost out here. They were almost at John and Catherine's house. 'Twas

too far from home. He'd never be able
find his way back or survive the
journey alone.

She pulled on her horse's reins,
she couldn't travel any farther
without her dog. "Scolty," she called
in a low voice. Fear of detection
prickled the hairs on the back of her
neck. "Scolty."

She heard a high-pitched bark.
Blood rushed out of her limbs. He'd
been hurt. She turned her horse, and
when her dog barked again, she knew in
which direction to go.

*Please, God, keep Scolty
uninjured.*

The moment she spotted him she
gasped. She needed more help from God
than she had time to pray for. Scolty
whined when she jumped down from her
horse. And as she ran to his side all
she saw was blood—Lachlan's blood.

Her dog had found him in a ditch.
His hat was nowhere to be seen, but he
still clung to his weapons. She
imagined he had used his musket as a
cane to drag his body here.

She wished to cry, to scream, but
that shan't help, 'twould only bring

trouble. She must tend to him. She was his only hope.

"Lachlan." She longed for him to answer her. He must be alive. "Lachlan." She bent down and stroked his wet hair.

Brown eyes rolled up to look at her. "Fiona?" He smiled. "My beautiful, Fiona," he rambled. "I must have died in battle."

"Nay, Lachlan. You're not dead." She ran her hand along his cheek. "You're wounded. Do you know where you're injured?" She prayed he hadn't been pierced or shot in the chest. Nothing could save him if he had.

His eyes held hers. Tears stung them. "I cannot move my left arm. I was stabbed with a bayonet in the shoulder." She thanked God, but knew this wound could be just as fatal if infection set it. And she didn't know how long he had been laying in this ditch. *God, please keep him alive.*

"Do you feel pain anywhere else?" She looked over the length of his body. He started to shake his head, but cried out in agony. "You cannot stay here. We must transport you home.

You need a doctor." She tried to move him, but he weighed much more than she. "Please, you must help me. You must mount my horse."

He leaned heavily on her as she pulled him to his feet. "We must hurry," she encouraged him, for if she was correct, the British had won and his life lay very much in danger still.

"Only a few more steps." She leaned him against her horse. How would she ever hoist him into the saddle? "Lachlan, you must depart from here immediately. Please tell me you understand?" She didn't know if he had comprehended anything she had said. His eyes rolled in and out of consciousness.

"Aye." He turned into her horse, and with more strength than she thought he possessed, he stepped onto a fallen tree trunk and raised himself into the saddle. Then he collapsed forward onto her horse's mane.

She offered Scolty a quick pat on his side. "Good dog." She jumped up behind Lachlan, and held him, along with the reins, as they raced home.

God, please heal him. She repeated those words more than she could count, for she knew not how to mend him.

"We ought to arrive shortly." She recited a verbal monologue and stroked his forehead every so often to keep him awake. He never uttered a word. But from the guttural sounds he spewed, she knew he suffered excruciating pain, and being jostled on her horse only heightened his agony. "Stay with me, Lachlan." She rubbed his back. "We shall be home soon."

She had never been so glad to set eyes upon her homestead. Fort George must wait. Her homestead stood closer and she wished him off her horse. He suffered terribly and she desperately feared for his life. He must lay down.

Halting Hope close to her entrance door, she climbed down first, then reached up to hold him as his body slumped toward the ground. Years of farm work had rendered her strong, but she still couldn't carry him.

"Lachlan, we must move you indoors." He forced his legs to

progress forward. "You can rest on the sofa in the drawing room." His chin dipped slightly.

She knew not where his strength came from, but she prayed 'twould last as they ambled into the house, one agonizing step after another. "Almost there." She helped him lower himself onto her sofa and then raised his legs to lie him down. "You accomplished this remarkably well. I am most proud of you." She covered him with a quilt. His eyes tightened shut from the pain.

"You need some refreshment." She dashed into the kitchen and her hands shook as she poured water. He had grown weaker. He needed more help than she could offer. He wouldn't survive much longer in this state.

She bounded back into the other room. His eyes lay shut. "Lachlan! Wake up!" His hazy brown orbs met hers and she brought the glass to his lips. "You must drink."

"Thank you," he barely murmured. She dipped her chin and brushed his hair away from his forehead. His skin burned.

Tears threatened to burst forth, but she fought them. 'Twouldn't do him any good to see her cry. She must provide him with hope. But his eyes shut once more and panic seized her. She stared at his chest. It rose and fell, but his breathing appeared labored. Unless she undertook to treat his wound herself, which she knew she could not, she needed to find someone who could.

Think, she yelled at herself. Fort George stood eleven kilometers away. That now seemed like a continent away. And besides, his comment yesterday had left her with the impression that the surgeon at the fort lacked the skill to handle a wound this severe.

But then who else could she involve in this situation? She was a British woman with an injured American officer in her home. One she had saved from a battlefield. She couldn't trust just anybody with that knowledge.

But she must find someone. She had no other choice. "I shall return as quickly as I can." She stood

knowing of only one person who could
help—Doctor Edgar Blackstone.

*F*iona raced to the doctor's house. She prayed the entire way that somehow God would arrange for him to come to Lachlan's aid. *Please, God, let him be home.* The heat of the late afternoon sun bore down on her as she knocked on his door.

Relief had never been an emotion she had felt in the presence of the doctor, but at this moment, as she looked into his confused expression, that is exactly what she felt.

"Fiona?" His dark eyes narrowed on her. "Why have you come?"

"I came to speak with you." She held her hands together and tried to appear calm. "May I enter?"

"Certainly." He opened the door wider and allowed her to walk past him into a large vestibule. "My cousin informed me she had met you in town this morning."

"Aye, I happened upon Mrs. Johnson at the butcher's shop."

"My cousin also mentioned that she told you I'm a forgiving man." He motioned for her to step into his drawing room. His house and furnishings were exceedingly grand. "I wish to assure you that she's correct. Please, sit."

He seated himself in an identical upholstered chair opposite hers. "Is that the reason why you've come? Has your opinion toward our marriage changed?" His tone grew almost pleasant, as if he were a truly compassionate man.

"Nay." The word had barely escaped her lips, before he sprung to his feet. "I've come on a different purpose." She rose, as well. No matter how scared she became of him, she shan't allow him to intimidate her. She had come here for Lachlan. "I need your assistance."

"You require my help?" He laughed. "And what, pray tell, do you need me to assist you with?" He stepped before her in front of an expansive hearth and didn't allow her an opportunity to answer. "If I disgust you to the point that you could never be impressed upon to marry me, whatever would compel you to ask me for help? Nay, better still, why should I help you when you stand with such opposition to marrying me?" He snarled and crossed his arms.

She took a deep breath, then strained her neck to look up at him. "You're a doctor. That is your life's work. 'Tis what you excel at. I am merely here to request that you use your medical skills to save someone's life."

His eyebrows shot up. "You appear healthy to me. Hence, who may I ask is this other person that requires assistance?"

"I cannot confide in you until you promise to help me."

He laughed again. The shrillness disconcerted her. "How can you deem me unsuitable as a husband, but yet find me worthy enough to keep your secrets?"

She turned away from him and walked to a window with its brocade curtains drawn. His land looked directly toward her own. "I shall disclose every detail. I promise. But first, you must vow to help me, and provide me with your assurance that you shall never tell another person what has transpired between us."

"And why, pray tell, must I do such a thing?"

This conversation had not advanced the way she had hoped. Time was being wasted. Time Lachlan did not have. She turned her gaze back into the ornate, but cheerless room. "I can pay you. I possess money." Her dream of breeding horses must wait. "How much do you require?"

He flashed her a grin. "Pay me? Oh, Fiona—" he shook his head as he stepped toward her "—I don't covet your money."

Oh, dear God, shall I be obliged to marry him to save Lachlan's life? "But money is all I'm willing to offer you."

"Then, my sweet." He pushed a strand of her hair behind her ear. She stiffened with repulsion at his touch. "My answer must be—nay."

"Nay?" His answer couldn't be nay. She couldn't allow Lachlan to die. "What must I do to persuade you? Pray tell, what do you desire?"

His grin grew. "What I've always wished for." Her hands clutched her stomach. It ached at the thought of being married to, or more precisely, owned by, Edgar. "Your land, Fiona."

Her eyes widened. "Please, Edgar, be reasonable. 'Tis my home. Surely you possess no need for my land. Would you not rather gain by having more money? You could build onto this house, add to your collections, purchase another tapestry," she stammered to find more uses for the money.

"That land was promised to me long before your aunt married my uncle and you wormed your way into his good graces," he sneered. "I still cannot comprehend how, or why, you inherited his homestead. But aside from the material gain, I am attached to that land. Sure, my cousin is alive, but like you, I don't have any immediate family. Hence, of all people, you ought to understand my attachment to that homestead. That land is all that remains of my heritage."

She swallowed hard. Seeing Lachlan again was akin to forging a connection to her past. His presence brought back a multitude of memories. If her land meant that much to the doctor, then aye, she did indeed know why he had become obsessed with acquiring her homestead.

"If I sign over my land to you, do you promise to help my friend, and never, ever, under any circumstance, speak of this matter to anyone?"

A gleam lit his dark eyes. "Aye."

"You answered in haste. This matter is of vital importance. You do realize you must take my secret to your grave?"

"I would do anything for that land. And contrary to what you think of me, I'm not a monster. I am a man of my word."

She could only pray he spoke the truth, for she had no other option. Lachlan would die without the aid of a doctor. He needed his wound tended to—now. "Fine, Edgar. The land shall be yours after you help my friend."

The widest grin spread across his face. "Thank you, and I do believe this is for the best, considering what people now think of you, you would no longer be comfortable living here. You shall be happier elsewhere."

She wiped her forehead. She hadn't thought that far ahead. She had only concerned herself with obtaining the help Lachlan needed. Where would she live after she parted with her land? "I appreciate your concern, but let us not waste any more time in discussion. We must depart for my home posthaste."

"I beg your pardon, but you may as well become accustomed to referring to it as *my home*?"

"Fine," she grunted. "Now if you shall be so kind as to grab your medical instruments and supplies so we may leave."

He nodded with a pompous smile. "It may be of benefit to me if you tell me of your friend's condition, then I shall know precisely what I ought to bring." He walked to the door. "Is your friend birthing a baby out of wedlock?" he called over his shoulder.

"My friend is an American officer." He spun on his heel and they stared at one another. *Please, God, don't permit him to change his mind.* "He's been stabbed in the left shoulder with a bayonet. He's already lost an abundance of blood, and he keeps bleeding—" she rambled out the details of how she had found him and brought him home.

"My you've brought more mayhem into your life these past two days than most people do in a lifetime?" He shook his head, then set about gathering his medical tools. "I thought the rumors circulating around town regarding you were terrible, but this—" he stopped to behold her "—this is treason. You could be brought to trial and put to death."

She swallowed the lump in her throat. "That shall never happen though, because no one, aside from you, has any knowledge of this." She glared at him. "But now you understand my need for secrecy."

"Aye." He closed his medical bag. "And don't fret. As long as you uphold your side of our arrangement, I shan't tell anyone."

*   *   *

Fiona ushered Edgar straight into the drawing room. Lachlan's chest still lifted and fell. *Thank You, God, for keeping him alive.*

"I shall require plenty of water." The doctor set his medical bag down and began to tend his patient.

She hesitated. "Please, assure me you can save him."

He glanced at her. "All I know for certain is that this man's fortunate you know the best surgeon in Upper Canada, for even though I cannot guarantee he shall live, I remain his best chance at survival."

She hoped Edgar's conceit stood well-founded, for one final look at Lachlan revealed just how pale and weak he had become. *God, please heal him.*

After she had fetched the water and brought it to Edgar, she assembled the ingredients for soup and set it on the hearth to cook. The door was now closed to her drawing room. She repeated a stream of prayers whilst she paced, and only paused when Lachlan screamed in pain. He was alive though, she told herself, not to have heard him would have been worse. Nevertheless, she still cried at each wail.

When the drawing room door finally creaked open, she rushed to search for the results on Edgar's face, for she stood completely unable to voice the only question on her mind—would Lachlan live?

"He's weak. He didn't succumb to a stab wound in the shoulder with a regular bayonet, the one that pierced him was triangular." The doctor ran his hand through his dark tousled hair, but it didn't soothe the locks, instead they appeared even more haggard.

"I shan't expect you to understand this, but a triangular cut, such as the one he obtained, is more than merely difficult to sew back together. Lesser skilled surgeons don't possess the mastery to close such a wound. Many merely amputate every injury. But fortunately for him, I do possess such skill." He stood tall, and crossed his arms as he looked down his nose at her.

"Had the wound been several inches to the right, your American officer would have been struck through the heart. He would have died immediately."

She nodded and hugged herself to ward off the tremors that shook her body. *Thank You, God.*

"Now, if he does survive, I cannot say for certain whether he shall ever have the use of his left arm again."

Her hand covered her mouth. *Oh, Lachlan.*

"You must persist in making him partake in food and drink. He's lost an excessive amount of blood." The doctor rolled down his shirtsleeves. "I've bandaged him, but he shall need your prayers to assure that infection shan't set in."

"But he's alive." She clung to that fact. "So, God-willing, he shall recover."

The doctor looked up and struck her with his glare. "Don't deceive yourself. He's barely in this life. And if infection sets in, he shall die. Nevertheless, I shall remain here for the night and tend him."

"Thank you." She was resolved to hold on to hope. "Please, permit me to serve you some soup." She led him into the kitchen and ladled broth into a bowl, then brought some to Lachlan.

She didn't think it possible, but his face had grown even paler. She pulled a chair beside the sofa and stroked his warm forehead. His eyelids fluttered open and she smiled. "I'm pleased to see those beautiful brown eyes." He didn't respond. Not even a grunt. He must be exhausted.

"I've brought you soup to aid your recovery." She held the spoon to his lips and encouraged him to partake in some nourishment. "Your shoulder has been treated. Now you must fight to regain your strength." She continued to feed him until he had eaten as much as he could. "Rest." She stroked her fingers through his damp hair, and immediately, he fell into a deep sleep.

In the kitchen, she found Edgar. And by the level of broth left in her pot, he had helped himself to another bowl or two. "Lachlan's asleep."

"Good. He shall require an ample amount of rest." The doctor rose. "You ought to eat and then rest yourself.

There is naught you can do for him now. I shall remain with him, and if he awakes, I shall see to his needs."

She dipped her chin. "Thank you."

She'd silence her stomach, then tend her animals, but as for sleep, that was highly unlikely, and she shan't last the entire night without a glimpse at whether Lachlan had improved.

*   *   *

Lachlan awoke from the sound of the doctor snoring. His right hand went instinctively to his left shoulder. The pain roared with ferocity. Although it hurt much less now then when the doctor had worked on him.

He searched the room for Fiona. She wasn't there. Disappointed, his eyes rested on the dark night sky. She had probably gone to sleep. *Thank You, God, for sending her to save my life. Although, I cannot fathom how she found me.* Had she gone in search of him, or had she merely found him on her way elsewhere? Whichever, he had become an unbearable burden to her. Bedridden, in what now must be enemy territory, he ought not remain in her house. If someone found him, the repercussions would prove disastrous, for them all.

He shan't put her in danger. He must leave. Now. He sat up. The room spun. He fell back. *God, You must give me the strength.* He tried again. *Please, God.* But he failed.

He lay still, unable to move. First opportunity that presented itself he'd be gone.

*   *   *

With a glass of water for Lachlan, Fiona left the kitchen and walked to the drawing room. She prayed he'd be awake. She had checked on him constantly yesterday, but he had slept the entire day.

Edgar had been in and out, as well, but she had avoided him. However, to-day, that wasn't possible. "Good morning." He emerged from the drawing room.

"Good morning." She peered past him and saw Lachlan asleep. "Has he improved?" she kept her voice low.

"He's still asleep. But his shoulder is healing."

"That's wonderful." The heaviness in her heart lightened a wee bit. "Do you care for tea before you depart? As usual, everything is laid out on the kitchen table." He dipped his chin and plodded into the next room.

She entered the drawing room, and her heart jolted when Lachlan stirred. "How do you feel?" she asked the moment his eyelids opened.

"I've been better," his voice rang hoarse.

She laughed, then held the glass of water to his lips. "I've been praying for your recovery, and it seems God has answered my prayers. Even if He took it upon Himself to infuse you with more humor."

He chuckled. "Please don't give me cause to laugh." His hand sought his shoulder.

"I apologize." She leaned forward with concern.

He shook his head. "Nay, you must never apologize to me." She fumbled with the glass in her hands. "If you didn't find me, I would have died. I owe you my complete gratitude."

She glanced her downcast eyes up at him. "Then we shall thank, God, because it is He who led me to you, or—" she grinned "—more precisely, He led Scolty to you. I told you my dog loves you."

He matched her grin. "A wee morsel of food convinced him most easily."

"'Twas more than the biscuits." She grew bold. "My dog is equipped with a good sense of people." His brown eyes deepened. She looked away at the window. "When you're well enough, I shall transport you to Fort George."

"You've already put yourself in an excessive amount of danger for me. I shan't concede to anymore. I shall depart to-day."

Her jaw dropped and her head jerked to face him. "But you're not well enough to travel yet, and when you are, I shan't permit you to travel alone."

"Fiona," his stern use of her name made her stomach clench.

Why was he in such a hurry to be rid of her? Nay, he shan't reject her friendship. His need to protect her, even as he lay injured, endeared him to her even more. "Lachlan, I've helped you thus far, and I shan't cease my efforts until you're completely well and safe, understood?"

He grinned at her. "I suppose I'd do well not to argue?"

"Aye, then I can conclude your good sense is still fully intact." She laughed along with him, but then grew serious. "I couldn't save anyone in my family, but I shall save you."

His eyes held hers and the need to look away overtook her. He patted her hand. She knew he understood. "Fort George is near enough that I don't suppose any harm shall befall you if you transported me." He pushed himself up. "What does your doctor think about everything that has transpired?"

My doctor? She didn't understand his choice of words. "If you're worried he shall tell someone your whereabouts, you need not. He shan't disclose our secret." Not if he wishes this homestead. Her eyes roved about the room—her drawing room—which would indeed be Edgar's soon enough. All of this would.

"I owe him my thanks."

She held in a snicker. She couldn't admit what she had done. If he thought a straightforward trip to Fort George was an imposition, he'd be infuriated that she had given her homestead to Edgar in exchange for his help.

"I've thanked him enough for both of us." He dipped his chin, but his eyebrows pinched together. However, she wouldn't explain. "I shall prepare something for us to eat." She stood.

"Thank you." He reached out and squeezed her hand.

She pulled up her closed lips into what she hoped looked akin to a smile. "'Tis unnecessary for you to thank me given all you've done for me since your regiment captured my homestead. And besides, we're friends. And where I hail from, friends help each other." She winked at him, then hurried to the kitchen. "Edgar!" She seethed, the moment she crossed the threshold. "What new impertinence is this?"

He didn't falter, and continued to rifle through one of her cupboards. "Just perusing what I shall be taking possession of shortly."

"I agreed to relinquish my homestead. The land. Not all its contents."

A look of amused astonishment settled on his face. "I wasn't aware of those limitations. Hum—" he rubbed his chin "—this changes things."

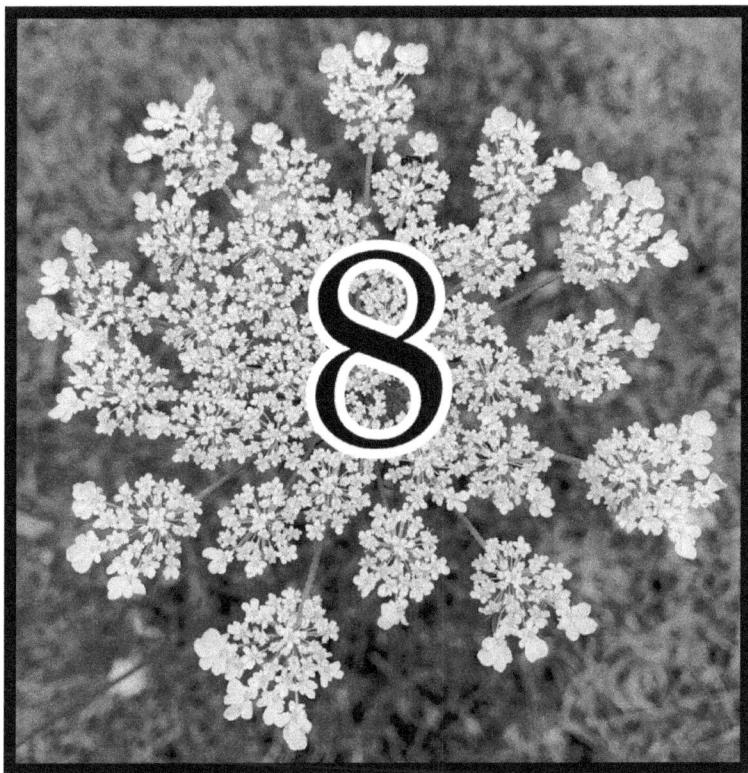

*E*xplain yourself, Edgar."
Fiona strode past him and
began to fix breakfast.
For now, this was still
her kitchen.

"We had an
agreement. But if you've changed your
mind—" he drawled out the last bit.

"I haven't changed my mind," she snapped.

"Good, because 'twould be most unfortunate for you, and your American officer, if your situation became known."

She lost the grip on the bowl she held and it slammed to the floor. He must have foreseen this. He could lie about why he had helped, but she'd be tried for treason and Lachlan would be taken as a prisoner of war, or killed. "Are you threatening me?"

"By no means." A sinister smile overtook his face.

She remained paralyzed. "You promised not to speak of this to anyone."

"And I shall uphold my promise—" he dipped down and grabbed the bowl "—but only *if, you* uphold yours." He offered her the wooden vessel whilst his dark eyes pierced hers. She snatched the wood from his hand and her stomach twisted, as if her acceptance of his gesture gave him authority over her.
Undaunted by the fury she exuded, he smiled. "When you pronounced this

homestead mine, you never stipulated
that your offer didn't include all it
encompassed."

"You couldn't possibly desire
everything." She swung the bowl about
and motioned at her possessions.

"Nay?" He arched a brow.

Had the bowl been made of
porcelain, she would have crushed it
in her bare hands. "You possess no use
for my clothing or other personal
items. Nor do you possess any
sentimental attachment to anything I
brought here from my childhood in the
United States."

"I agree." He dipped his chin as
if he were the most agreeable man in
Upper Canada. "'Tis not my intention
to stow away as a thief. I shan't
steal from you. I'm just merely taking
possession of what's rightfully mine.
And to prove it. I shall even permit
you to maintain possession of your
dog."

"Thank you," she said through
gritted teeth. Did he believe he had
fooled her? She knew he despised her
dog. "As soon as Lachlan is well
enough, we shall ride off your land."

She recommenced her breakfast
preparations with renewed fury.

"I beg your pardon?" He blocked
her ability to work. "I dare say I
must have heard you incorrectly,
because I believe you said, *ride off*,
my land? Are you planning on riding
your dog?"

She stared at him. Nay, she
shan't allow this to come to pass. "I
shall take my horse. He's mine. He was
never part of this homestead." Her
fists clenched tighter than her teeth.

"I beg to differ. That animal has
been living on this land, consuming
its harvest for years. 'Tis as much a
part of this homestead, as the other
farm animals I shall acquire."

"Nay." Her blood boiled. "Hope is
coming with me."

"*Hope*?" He smirked. "For your
sake, I *hope* they are unusually lax
when they discover what you've done."

"Edgar—"

"Fiona, I don't espy any reason
to continue this discussion. I refuse
to argue with you. Your choice is
clear, either you transfer this
homestead to me, with *all* its

contents, save your personal items and that mongrel, or you intentionally break our agreement, knowing full well what the consequences shall be."

Her mind raced for a way to save her quarter horse from his clutches. If he took her horse her dream of breeding horses would be over before it began. She stammered, but her mouth didn't generate an appeal. "You win," she resigned. Lachlan's life was more precious to her than anything. She'd be grateful to God for providing her with the means to save him. Nevertheless, she stormed out of the house and ranted under her breath the entire way to her water-well.

Once she filled a bucket, she returned with the heavy burden to the kitchen. Before she could even pour the liquid into a pot, her muscles tightened into rock at the sound of Edgar's voice behind her. "I just tended to Lachlan and I believe he's strong enough to leave."

Her hands stilled. Did he actually believe Lachlan was well enough or did he merely wish them dislodged?

"I shall return later for the property patent and I expect you to have written a note that states your willingness to bestow the land to me. And please—" he jeered "—don't forget your signature."

"I shan't." The bucket hit the floor with a thud. "Wait." She wished nothing more than for him to leave, but she had questions that needed answers. "How long before Lachlan's shoulder heals completely?"

"Only God knows for certain. But 'tis mending, and once the medication I administered abates, he ought to feel more himself." He stepped back toward the door. "I do expect him to recover fully, especially now that he moved his left hand."

Her fingers flew to her heart. "Thank You, God."

"Ahem," Edgar coughed.

"Was there something else?" She raised her eyebrows.

"Nay." A grin spread across his face. "There's no need for you to thank me with *words*. This homestead is all the thanks I desire." He laughed as he walked out.

* * *

"Edgar informed me of your favorable prognosis." Fiona sat in the chair next to Lachlan on the sofa.

"Aye." He forced a smile.

"You don't believe him?" She stirred the steaming bowl of soup in her hand.

He shrugged his good shoulder. "I pray he's correct, but he couldn't tell me how long until I fully recover."

She gave him a tight smile. "I understand your frustration, but God's timing is never wrong. Remember Ecclesiastes, *To every thing there is a season, and a time to every purpose under the heaven.* Now here, eat. It shall only hasten your rehabilitation."

"Aye, ma'am," he teased, and she knew he didn't wish to dwell on his disgruntlement. He ate in amicable quiet. "Thank you," he said once he had finished.

"My pleasure." She smiled. "I'm glad your appetite has returned." She stood, but didn't step toward the door. Her eyes remained on the spoon she moved around in the empty bowl. "I shall rummage through my uncle's trunk to look for clothes that may fit you."

"Thank you." He peered down at his blood stained attire. "I'd be much obliged to arrive at Fort George without drawing unwanted attention with these soiled clothes."

She grinned, then left the room to steady herself. This task involved more than merely choosing clothes. 'Twould be the last time she'd sort through her belongings before she left nearly all of them behind.

Emotions flooded her and she avoided the chore by first packing some food. She shed countless tears before she dropped her valise by the entrance door and returned to the drawing room with an armful of clothes.

"I hope these fit." She laid the garments over the chair next to the sofa. "If not, I shall rummage through my uncle's trunk once more. I have towels and a warm pitcher of water

waiting in the kitchen, with some soap
if you care to wash."

"Thank you." Gratitude shone from
his eyes as his legs swung over the
cushioned edge. "You must have many
things to attend to before we depart.
I shall come help you once I'm
dressed."

She shook her head. "I cannot
accept your help this time. You still
need rest, and we have a long day
ahead." Exceedingly long, if she added
finding a new place to live, because
after she took him to Fort George, she
knew not where she'd sleep
tonight—let alone live out the rest
of her days.

He stood, and his hand shot to
his forehead. "If you're not feeling
well enough, we can postpone our
departure." She'd fight Edgar if she
must.

"Nay." He didn't hesitate. "The
sooner we leave the better." He picked
up the clothes and bowed out of the
room.

The sting from his words rang in
her ears. They'd be parted forever in
a matter of hours. She sighed as she

bent down to roll back the braided oval rug. The loose floor plank came up with ease. She lifted her secret sack out and a wee jewelry box that held some sentimental trinkets she hadn't sold. Then, she reached back into the hidden compartment for her homestead's patent.

After she replaced the plank, and rug, she took the patent to her desk. With her quill dipped in the inkwell, she offered a prayer to God, then wrote the note Edgar had insisted upon. However, after she signed the letter, she wrote him a second note. One he was certainly not expecting.

Edgar,
I am aware that as part of our agreement you requested this homestead, and all its contents, but I must take my Quarter Horse to-day. I need him to carry Lachlan and myself to Fort George. I believe the walk would prove detrimental to Lachlan.

Afterward, I shall need my horse to search for somewhere else to live, since I cannot return here. But please be

assured that once I have found a
place to lay my head for the
night, I shall leave my horse in
a nearby stable and send word so
you may collect him.
     I hope you understand the
necessity of my actions.
     Fiona Robertson

     In disbelief, she stared at the
words she had written. This homestead
no longer belonged to her. She'd never
see her animals after to-day.
     Except for her dog, she smiled
down at the white and sable collie
that had just panted into the room.
"You're the only one keeping me from
being alone in this world." She gave
him a rub. "Come, we must banish these
sorrowful thoughts. There's work to
do." He bounded out of the room beside
her, with more enthusiasm than she
possessed. She couldn't help but run
her hand along the bumpy wall trying
to put to memory every detail of her
homestead.

                *   *   *

Lachlan took more time to dress
than he had ever taken in his life,
thanks to his every movement sending a
wave of pain crashing over him.

But he had imposed on Fiona long
enough. She didn't need the additional
burden of taking care of him. And she
certainly didn't need to be in the
throes of danger by housing the enemy.

When he finally dragged himself
out of the kitchen, he sauntered past
the drawing room. It lay empty. She
was probably in the barn. He headed
for the entry door and noticed a
valise and an open bag with food. Why
had she packed so much just to
accompany him to Fort George? He knew
not as he stepped out of doors.

The day had progressed into
another hot haze, and he found her in
the stable saddling up Hope. "Are you
set to depart?" he asked, before he
saw her tears.

"Just about." She whirled away
and swatted at the wetness that
streamed down her cheeks.

He didn't move. He couldn't. If
her tears were due to his
departure—nay, that couldn't be the

reason. She didn't harbor feelings for him. "Care to confide in me?"

"I'm fine." She turned with a smile pasted on her lips. "Are you ready?" He nodded. "Then, we ought to leave."

She led her horse out of the stable, and her dog ran circles around them. "I'm glad my uncle's clothes fit." Her hazel eyes glanced over him, but he doubted she saw anything besides her younger brother's best friend.

"Aye, thank you again for offering them to me." She nodded, and settled her gaze on her home. His fingers played with the sling that held his left arm across his chest.

"I shall retrieve the bags." She disappeared within, and he led her stallion to a bench so he could mount the horse more easily.

When she returned, she strapped the bags on Hope, then climbed into the saddle. "I thought it may be better if I sat behind you, so you can hold onto Hope's mane if need be." She turned the horse.

"Thank you." He glanced over his shoulder at her. "Do you not loathe riding astride?"

"Nay, and please don't mention that 'tis unladylike, for I can list a myriad of women who prefer to ride this way." With a smirk, she counted on her fingers. "The Empress of Russia, Catherine II, the former queen of France, Marie Antoinette—"

"Fair enough." He laughed, but her humor died when her eyes roved over her homestead.

"Ready?" her voice cracked behind forlorn features. He remained quiet for a moment with wonder at why she seemed to look upon her land as if she'd never see it again.

"Aye," he answered. He had to return to his military life, where he belonged. But his eyes slammed shut when the horse's gait jostled his shoulder.

"Sorry." She grimaced, and took care to choose a steady path as she rode Hope at a slow canter. The kilometers passed. But despite her efforts, his shoulder injury was simply too new and the pain was immense.

"Lachlan, do you hear that?"

He looked about for the source of the noise. "It sounds like horses galloping, but I don't see any."

"How odd, because 'twould have to be a rather large team to create such a din." She kept her eyes on the path. "Could the British be on their way to attack Fort George?"

Despite the soreness, he leaned to peer behind them. A cloud of dust floated into the horizon. "If that is British cavalry, we need to remove ourselves from this path." She nodded. "Wait." He squinted. "I see the doctor."

"It cannot be." Her head jerked around to look. "God, help us." She loosened the reins and her Quarter Horse set off like the racehorse he was. "Scolty, run!"

Shots of pain fired through him. "Why do we flee?" he yelled.

"Because it appears Edgar's riding with the whole town of Queenston." She beckoned her horse to move faster.

"I don't understand," he blurted. If she was about to marry the doctor then why would she run from him?

"I believe he revealed our secret."

"What?" His body numbed. "Why would he betray your confidence?"

"Because I took his horse." Her attention centered on making Hope accelerate with accurate agility.

"*His* horse?"

"Aye. *His* horse." Anger tinged her words. "Please trust me to explain later. For now, I must concentrate on reaching Fort George before they capture us."

With his shoulder throbbing, Lachlan held fast to the horse's mane. But there was no relief from the pain, or the questions that circled in his mind. He was certain Fiona had told him Hope was her horse and she planned to breed him.

"Alas, there's Fort George," he shouted, the moment the palisade came into view. She charged toward it. The wind whirled past them and dust muddled the air as Hope's hooves pounded the earth.

"Wait, look," he yelled. "They're slowing their pace."

She thrust her head around. "Thank You, God."

"You must reduce our speed, as well, Fiona." She stared at him with uncertainty. "With these clothes, I shall be mistaken for the enemy, and the Brigadier General shall issue a command to shoot us." She pulled up on the reins. "Guide Hope to the main gate." He pointed to a spot beside the dry ditch that surrounded the fort. She nodded apprehensively, but did as she was bid.

"They're retreating," he cheered. "We're safe now." But guilt gnawed at him. If it hadn't been for him, she wouldn't be here. He had ruined her life. "I assure you, I shan't allow any harm to befall you."

Somehow, he'd fix this.
But how?

Fiona sat on her horse and watched Lachlan approach the guards. He walked with confidence. As he should, she buried her head into Hope's neck. *He* belonged here. *She* however, was now a woman devoid of a country.

"Fiona." She peered around her horse's head and saw Lachlan wave her to him. With a call to her dog, she slid off Hope, then fastened a leash to Scolty's collar and led them forward. "Don't be bothered by the soldiers milling about, Fiona." The worry coursing through her veins must have been visible on her face. "You're safe here." He handed her horse's reins to a soldier, who allowed her to give her horse a final rub on the head and a kiss on his muzzle before he led him away.

She squeezed Scolty's leash to her chest, and unease gripped her as they entered the massive fort with blue coats performing various duties everywhere she looked.

As she studied her surroundings, she clutched her valise tighter, and stayed close to Lachlan, who held the bag of food.

The outer walls of wooden stakes shot up from the ground like enormous arrows that heightened to the clouds and stretched as far as the eye could see. Every so often there were holes dug through the timber where guards watched for approaching signs of trouble.

Buildings of all sizes and shapes were littered throughout a sea of well trampled grass and dirt. The green and brown ground rose into small hills, mostly around the edges, and the six corner points where cannons loomed. All the structures were built of wood, except one stone house near the back of the fort that blocked the view of a tunnel.

They'd passed many women and children, and yet, even seeing that she wasn't the only female behind these towering walls failed to calm her. "Why are those women and children distraught?"

In hushed tones, he replied, "Those are the families of the men that didn't survive the battle." His fingers played with the hem of his sling. "Whilst you waited with Hope, I spoke to the guards about my experience."

She reached out and rubbed his arm. She knew he suffered with them. *God, please give them comfort.* She held back the tears that the bereaved could not. If anything had happened to Lachlan—

"Shall we rest by the palisade and refresh ourselves." He held up her bag of food. "There's shade."

She dipped her chin. "Some relief from this heat would be most welcome." She pulled out her fan and sent a breeze over to him.

He closed his eyes with a content expression. "Pure bliss."

She chuckled and held her fan out to him. "You may fan yourself whilst I position my gown properly beneath me."

"I think not." He grimaced at the lacy feminine article. "But I do apologize for asking you to sit upon the ground. I just assumed you'd prefer the solitude over the commotion of the officer's quarters. Was I mistaken?"

She shook her head and patted the smooth blades of grass beside her. He sat and took a towel full of food from the bag. "Thank you." His grin widened once he had unfolded the material. "Your biscuits are delicious." He smelled them, then offered them to her.

She took two, gave one to her dog and then managed to take a wee bite of the other. Her nerves had ruined her appetite. However, without the knowledge of where her next meal would come from, or when she'd enjoy it, her head began to pound, and she forced herself to eat that biscuit and several more.

Stealing a glance at him, she noticed something she hadn't before, something he had concealed under his smile. But now, when he thought she wasn't watching, his face drooped in sorrow. He must be lost in the thought of whatever tormented him. Perhaps the widows, his shoulder, or was she to blame?

She shifted uncomfortably on the grass. She hadn't meant to become a burden. But one thing she knew for certain was that she wouldn't remain one. As soon as 'twas feasible, she'd embark on a new life. Perhaps move to a city and find work as a seamstress or a laundress. She was young and healthy. She'd do whatever was required to fulfill her dream of breeding horses.

"Fiona." He interrupted her thoughts.

"Aye?"

"I still cannot comprehend why the doctor betrayed you, but I do know that in doing so, he rendered it impossible for you to remain in Upper Canada."

She nodded. "Do you suppose I shall be allowed to live in the United States?"

"You were born an American, so in my opinion you shall always be one. That is, if you wish to be. But, if not, there are plenty of other countries around the world where you could happily settle."

"True." Her gaze fell to her empire waist gown. She knew she walked this earth alone, without any ties to a specific place. But somehow hearing him suggest as much, made her head pound anew. "How do you suppose I ought to leave Upper Canada? Must I travel to the United States first?"

"I've already attended to that matter. We shall be ferried across the Niagara River soon."

"We?" Her eyebrows pinched together.

"I've been dismissed." That look of sorrow crossed his face again. "Due to my injury."

"I'm sorry." She placed her hand over his.

"Seems as if we're both stepping into new lives."

She bit the inside of her cheek as she nodded, but it hurt even more to witness him suffer. "According to Edgar though, you are due to recover fully." She attempted to buoy his spirits. "And I'm certain you shall mend promptly."

"I hope in this case we may trust the doctor. Nevertheless, before we depart, if you don't mind waiting alone, I do indeed wish to visit with our surgeon."

"Certainly. I think that a fine idea."

*   *   *

"I apologize for the length of my examination, Lachlan. But this stitching is remarkable. Whoever performed this surgery was a master surgeon."

"Take as long as you need, doctor. It pleases me to know that my suffering may help you learn a skill that in turn may save more lives."

The doctor studied the wound even closer. "I am much obliged." He scribbled down plenty of notes and diagrams before he bandaged the wound anew. "I believe I shan't provide false hope in my agreement that you are indeed on your way to a complete recovery. But I do apologize that I cannot confirm the length of your recovery, and I think it only fair to mention that in all likelihood you shall carry the scar from this battle until your dying day."

He nodded. "I'm just grateful to be alive. Thank you, doctor." He shook the man's hand before he stepped out into the sunlight.

Fiona ran to him. Her wary words escaped in a rush, "What did you ascertain?"

"Doctor Blackstone is proficiently skilled." He was glad, but it irked him to praise the man. "I shall mend well."

"Wonderful." She clasped her hands together and touched them to her lips. "I'm utterly relieved."

He dipped his chin, but felt the complete opposite. "Sadly, 'tis encumbent upon me to convey some rather bad news to you." Her smile dissipated and he abhorred that it fell upon him to hurt her.

"Out with it." Her body stiffened and he thought she had stopped breathing. "Please."

He ran his fingers through his hair. "I've tried in vain to devise a gentle way by which to parlay this news to you. But, it has all come to

naught, and so I shall just say it."
He took a deep breath. "Your horse
must remain here."

Her shoulders slumped, but her
chest heaved, which reassured him that
she was once again breathing. "Please,
say something."

One of her hands rested on her
chest. "I feared you had something
more detrimental to inform me of." His
brows lifted and the tiniest smile
lifted her lips. "You see, I already
lost my horse, and I mourned him,
ergo, somehow losing him again fails
to cut as deep."

He wished her to offer further
explanation, but they were
interrupted. "Lachlan, 'tis time to
board the ferry," a soldier called. In
response, he raised his hand with a
wave.

"Scolty may still accompany us
though?" Worry pinched her brows.

"Aye." He smiled down at the
medium-sized dog that walked beside
them. "I'm very much inclined to treat
him as a hero."

"That he is." She patted him, and
his ears dipped down, while his tail

swished at the attention. "He did locate you."

"Because of you." She blushed, but he continued, "I shan't ever forget your conduct or the risk you braved for me."

"Oh, Lachlan—" She shook her head in disregard.

"Nay, Fiona. I shall thank you somehow. Someday."

*   *   *

"The United States of America." Fiona took a deep breath, after they had vacated the ferry at the foot of the bluff by Fort Niagara. "Smells akin to Upper Canada." Her head surveyed the terrain. "Appears similar, as well."

Lachlan laughed. "I cannot argue. These parts are similar."

"Aye." She stretched her neck back to cast her eyes upon the cloudless blue sky. "I'm free." She spun with glee, causing him to chuckle and her dog to bark. She stopped to pet Scolty. Her happiness faded. "War has waged for a solid year around my homestead. But, I suppose I'm still not free, am I?" He looked at her curiously. "I may not need to fret about the daily effects of war any longer, but I must map out a new life for myself, and that may bind me even more permanently."

"You needn't contemplate this now. Allow yourself time before you settle on a plan." He watched the flow of the river.

"I may have to heed your advice, because God created a big world." She swung out her arm. "Look at the vastness of the Niagara River. It's connected to Lake Ontario, which is connected to other waters and so on and so forth. The water floats on endlessly. My life is like a droplet of water now. I am adrift. I have no home, no family, no community, no roots, and no idea where I shall wind-up?"

"If the decision rested entirely with me, I would have us leave now to *wind-up* at my family's homestead before nightfall." She kicked at some dirt. "Please understand that I cannot leave you here alone." His fingers brought her chin up so she had to look into his pleading eyes. "Let me return your kindness and offer you some hospitality."

"That is a truly generous offer, but—I—" She looked past him to the stone walls of Fort Niagara.

"It shall please everyone to welcome you back."

She bit her lower lip. "That's precisely the problem. I know not if I can return. I fear I'm not ready to confront all the memories and emotions I left behind. Perhaps I may secure accommodation at a nearby inn?"

"Oh." He looked away at a bald eagle that soared overhead. Darkness shaded his features.

After being away for a year, he must be eager to return home. "I'd detest myself immensely if I kept you away from your family any longer though. And besides, you must allow your shoulder time to heal. So, if my accompanying you shall hasten your ability to rest happier and sooner, then I shall accept your invitation. As you said, I may plan my future from New Callander."

"Are you certain?" Concern edged the brown rings in his eyes. She dipped her chin, and he took her hand. "Remember, you're not alone. If you require a confident, someone to pray with, anything. I shall be more than happy to oblige."

"Thank you." She forced herself to smile.

His grin however, shone with true joy. "Come now, we must visit Fort Niagara first. I must speak with my superiors. Then I shall locate a carriage for our use." He held out his arm and she slid into place alongside him.

*   *   *

Lachlan pointed with his good arm. "There 'tis—" his smile spread from ear to ear "—home." Fiona sucked in a breath. "'Tis just as I remember it," he voiced her thoughts exactly.

Her homestead had lain directly beside his family's and there it still stood. It beckoned to her. She saw her mother beat dust out of a rug, while her father chopped wood, and her brother and Lachlan climbed the tall elm tree beside the drawing room window.

A teardrop fell, and then more followed. Unable to see past her tears, she slowed the horses to a halt. With a wipe at her cheek, she jumped down from the carriage. Shaken, she grabbed hold of her stomach and wrapped her arms around her waist to hold herself together. But the sobs ripped her apart.

An arm covered her shoulders and returned her thoughts to the present. He held her. She welcomed his support. She needed his strength.

Careful not to injure his shoulder she turned and cried into his chest.

Lachlan held Fiona as tight as his wound permitted. He shut his eyes and prayed. *God, guide me in helping her. For I seem to do nothing but cause her grief.* Her body trembled against him and he wished he had the use of both his arms to hold her more securely.

He looked down into her tear stained face. She wouldn't meet his eyes, but she didn't pull away. "I'm sorry," she whispered, in between the breaths she attempted to catch.

Her chest heaved as her weeping lessened. "You need not apologize. After your family perished you were whisked away without the opportunity to bid anyone farewell, let alone grieve." She dried the last of her tears. "I'm sorry I brought you here. I see now that I ought to have accompanied you to an inn."

She shook her head. "Nay, you need not blame yourself for *this*." She circled her hand around her mournful face. "I buried my memories and emotions for far too long. Even amidst my aunt and uncle I seldom mentioned my family or home. I feared they'd assume I disliked living with them or they'd deem me unappreciative."

He nodded and ran his hand over her hair. An imagine of her crying herself to sleep every night with no one to comfort her tore at his heart.

"I hope you consider me a confident. I shall always be here if you need me."

For a fleeting moment, red rimmed eyes sought his. "Thank you." She traipsed to the carriage. "We must not delay any longer though. We must see you home." She pulled herself up. "You do require rest. However, I anticipate a celebration before you lie down for the night."

The thought of beholding his family warmed him. "I do believe you to be correct." He climbed up beside her. "Are you certain you can manage this? There's bound to be talk of your family once we divulge your identity?"

"After this interlude, I'm no longer in possession of any more tears." She pushed her lips into a tight smile, before she called her dog back into the carriage and they set off.

The sun had set and the dim light from candles within his homestead shone.

Home.

A silly grin lit his face. He loved every iota of New Callander. And

now that he had returned, he couldn't
fathom how he had forced himself to
banish every thought about how much he
missed his life here.

*Thank You, God, for bringing us
home safely.*

Before they even reached the
yellow two-floor house, Lachlan's
parents emerged to investigate the
noise of their carriage. He waved his
good arm and she smiled at his
exuberance.

What would it feel like to be
lovingly received home by family? She
pushed the question away, she would
never have the pleasure of
experiencing that. But she did welcome
it for him. And she knew the moment
they had traveled close enough for his
parents to recognize him, because
merriment erupted into an otherwise
still night.

She stopped the horses and he
jumped down. With slow deliberation,
she disembarked, then came around the
horses to see his parents take turns
hugging and kissing him. She stood
back. Alone. Even her dog went to

greet the McAllister's black and white farm collie.

"And who is this lovely young lady?" Lachlan's father drew everyone's attention to her. "Did you marry?"

Heat rose to her cheeks. "You've taken a bride! Felicitations!" his mother covered her gaping mouth with one hand, and squeezed him tighter with the other. She hadn't released him since she had initially thrown her arms around him. "I'm overcome with happiness. I fear I shall cry."

"You're already crying, Maisie." Lachlan's father smirked.

"Oh, hush, Ennis." She swatted his arm playfully.

Lachlan interjected, "Sadly, this lovely young lady is not my wife." He left his parents and came to take her by the hand to bring her forward in introduction.

She swallowed the lump in her throat, even if he had only spoken in jest, his words sent pangs to her heart.

"May I introduce—" he squeezed her fingers "—or more precisely, *reintroduce*, Fiona Robertson."

Silence fell. The crickets flourished in their turn to speak again. "Fiona?" Maisie rushed to her. "Dear, sweet, kind, Fiona? I cannot believe my eyes. You're fully grown." His mother cupped her face. "We thought we had lost you forever. Oh, do come here." She enveloped her in a gracious hug. Fiona hugged her back. She had the fondest memories of her mother's dearest friend.

"I dare say you look remarkably akin to your mother." Her eyes began to well at the woman's affectionate words. Maisie smiled and patted her cheek. She must have understood her sentimentality. "I'm delighted you've come." She took Fiona's arm and clasped her hand over hers before she turned back to the men. "What an unexpected blessing. Truly, tonight is a prayer answered." She linked her other arm with her son's. "But let us not pass the entire night out of doors. Instead of allowing these mosquitoes to feast on us, I shall set out refreshments for us in the kitchen."

After they had stepped over the threshold into a charming vestibule, Maisie joined Fiona's arm to Lachlan's. "We shall start with tea." She grabbed her husband's hand and they hustled into the kitchen.

The smile on Lachlan's face still hadn't faded when he turned his radiance upon her. "Are you faring well?" he leaned in with a whisper.

His consideration nearly rendered her speechless. "Eminently well, thank you." She returned his smile with her own. "Please don't spend another moment with a fretful thought of me. I wish you to enjoy this."

He pulled her to him. "I wish you may enjoy it, as well."

The intimate gesture stayed with her long after they entered the kitchen, which was arranged in much the same manner as hers had been. But the amiable people within these walls created the coziest atmosphere. Even her wooden chair seemed to hug her, and she relished watching Lachlan throughout the evening, especially as she caught glimpses of his former self. The way he used to be, in their earlier years, before his military days, when life hadn't weighed on him.

"Shall I see you to your room, Fiona?" Maisie offered, once they had finished sampling her delectable provisions.

"Thank you." She stood to follow her. "I am much obliged at your generosity in having me to stay."

"'Tis our pleasure, my dear. But truth be told, 'tis Lachlan who ought to be obliged to you, because had he found you and failed to bring you home, well—'twould be most indelicate of me to speak of the repercussions he would have suffered."

They laughed, and as her eyes met his, amusement sparkled within them. "Indeed, you bestowed a most considerable favor upon me."

With a chuckle, she dipped her chin, then left him to speak with his father, as she followed his mother upstairs to a guest bedroom.

"Ennis thought to bring your valise up beforehand." Maisie pointed to a tripod candle table with a chair on each side that sat under the room's large white paned window. "Do you require anything further?"

"Nay, thank you. I shall be more than comfortable." She let her eyes roam over the pretty room adorned in walnut furniture. The four-poster bed was pushed into the left corner, and there was a small hearth on the opposite wall, with a mantelpiece that shelved two chamber candlesticks and books. The wallpaper was a striking emerald overlaid with a netting pattern, and the room's wood trim was painted white.

"Tomorrow, being Sunday, I do hope you shall consider attending church with us."

Church? She held onto a bedpost. She had plumb forgot that to-day was Saturday.

"There's to be a picnic afterward." Maisie pulled a cream blanket from one of the closets that flanked the hearth and placed it on the foot of the bed. "You ought to be able to reacquaint yourself with plenty of people you once knew."

Precisely what she feared. Her apprehension rose with the thought of how they had react to her. She couldn't endure the whispers—those words that still echoed in her head—*poor wretched orphan*.

"That's most kind of you to invite me, but—" She looked down at the wide wooden plank floor.

"Perhaps you ought to rest, dear." Maisie smiled, as if in some womanly, or perhaps motherly way, she had discerned her thoughts. "The morning shall bring a fresh beginning." She sauntered to the door. "Sleep well."

She nodded. "Good-night, and thank you."

Maisie smiled as she closed the door.

She looked about her once more, then set about the task of removing her night clothes from her valise. She laid them on top of the bed. However, instead of undressing, the window captivated her attention.

Her eyes rolled over the dimly lit countryside, and devoured the trees, pasture and farmland, until her

gaze settled on her childhood home.
She hugged herself and rubbed the
sleeves of her linsey-woolsey gown.

She wouldn't cry, she told
herself firmly. If this is how God
decreed her life, she must trust Him.
But, oh, how she missed her family.
She yearned to be among them. To
laugh, to talk, to embrace them, even
just once more.

A knock jerked her attention back
into the room. "One moment," she
called, as she scampered to open the
door. "Lachlan?" Her breath caught.

"I apologize if I've disturbed
you, but I thought perhaps you might
appreciate this." He handed her a
quilt. She glanced between the
variegated pattern and his expectant
face. "Now you understand why I was
affected by the one you had made for
your store."

"Lachlan—" she barely choked his
name past her lips "—this belonged to
my mother." She stroked the silk
medallion in the middle.

"Aye. Your mother presented it to
mine when we were children." As if in
need to find some employment for his

hands, he turned up a corner. "My parents were most grateful, and we made good use of it, but now we wish for you to possess it."

"I cannot possibly." She shook her head and held the patchwork out to him.

"We insist." With one hand he gently pushed the cotton material with wool filling back to her. "I hope it affords you comfort and brings you happiness."

"I adore it." She hugged the soft material. "I still remember my mother stitching these patches." She folded the quilt to show a segment that hadn't been sewn as neatly. "That's where, myself, and even my brother, endeavored to help her."

He tilted his head to examine the contours. "She would be proud to know you've finally learned to stitch straight."

She laughed through the tears that fell when she blinked. "I shall always cherish this. And not simply because 'tis one of the only things of my mother's that I own, but because you gave it to me. Thank you." She pulled down on his right shoulder to lower his head, then kissed his cheek.

The kiss had been one of spontaneous gratitude, but with her lips pressed against the rough stubble of his jaw, she paused. Something stirred in her. And the slight rise of his lips, did nothing to calm her rapidly accelerating pulse.

"I must remember to surprise you with presents more often," he chuckled, and sounded akin to his old self, the one she remembered with much fondness. But she had flamed up from the neck and couldn't even attempt a smile. "Sleep well." He stroked her arm, which created a new flurry of activity in her chest. She nodded. She didn't trust her voice when his chocolate eyes looked down at her so intently. "Goodnight." He withdrew his hand and then descended the stairs.

She slumped against the doorframe. 'Twould be harder to remain under this roof than she originally thought. Tomorrow, she'd begin her plans to leave—before it became impossible to say goodbye to New Callander again.

*L*achlan ambled into the kitchen. "Good morning, Mama."

"Good morning." She grinned. "I cooked oatmeal." He slipped into a chair at the table. "Your pa's out tending the animals before church." She set a steaming bowl of porridge before him.

He stirred it. "Life on a farm is indeed just as regimented as life in the military."

"I suppose so." His mother patted his hair. "Nevertheless, I'm overjoyed you're home. It does my heart good." She kissed the top of his head. "Oh, I forgot to mention, last night I invited Fiona to attend church with us. I hope you're feeling well enough to come, as well?" Her eyes rested on his left shoulder.

"Aye, Mama. I'm much improved." He didn't rub his sling until his mother had sauntered back to the hearth.

"I wonder when Fiona shall come down to breakfast?" She glanced at the open doorway. "But after the harrowing ordeal you both suffered I shan't dare wake her. And yet, if she doesn't come soon, she may miss church, and I did so hope she'd consent to join us."

So, Fiona hadn't agreed to attend church. He blew on a heaping spoonful of oatmeal. "She must be rather weary, for she's habitually an early riser."

He swished the grainy oats around in his mouth and plunged his spoon back into the creamy mush to avoid his mother's scrutiny. His words did ring peculiar, as if he knew her intimately. But he had just come from her home and couldn't expunge what he had noticed. "Alone on a homestead with countless animals, and a store, working all hours was a necessity," he rushed an explanation.

She turned from him to the other door. "Good morning, my dear." Her face spread into a smile, as Fiona entered from out of doors. "You must have quit the house before I even woke."

"Aye. I thought I'd tend the animals in the barn." She untied her bonnet. "However, once Mr. McAllister arrived, he insisted I not overtax myself, and unless I wished to invoke his ire, I had to agree to leave the remainder of the chores to him and partake in some breakfast."

"Then I'm glad you didn't vex him," he chuckled. "Pa is most adamant about putting the needs of others ahead of his own."

"Now I know from whom you acquired that trait." Her unexpected compliment jolted him more awake than coffee ever could.

She spun on her heel about to assist his mother, but she waved her away. "Please, sit. I shall serve you breakfast." His mother filled a bowl and retrieved another spoon.

She sat across from him. "You certainly have more animals than I did. How do you keep them all?"

"Usually help abounds." His mother set oatmeal before her.

"However, at the moment, our other children are visiting relatives."

She nodded. "Thank you. This smells delicious." His mother dipped her chin and returned to the hearth.

"How is Scolty faring?" he asked.

"I dare say he's rather fond of our being here. Besides the quickest of greetings this morning, he's been inseparable from your dog. I do believe I've been replaced as his companion of choice."

He laughed. "I apologize and shall speak with my furry friend."

"Thank you." She winked. "However, since I'm also faring rather well, I suppose we need not ruin their pleasurable diversions—just yet."

"Speaking of amusements, have you determined whether you shall attend church with us?" Lachlan's mother addressed her.

"Aye. I shall dress directly after breakfast."

"Wonderful." His mother grinned. "Are you in need of a gown? My lasses must have left one behind that ought to be to your liking."

"That's most kind. And even though I'm certain I would adore any one of your daughter's gowns, I do possess my own."

"Splendid." His mother beamed as she shed her apron. "With breakfast finished, I shall dress before Ennis requires something of me." Her smile reached her eyes as his mother patted her hair before she left.

When she glanced at him and caught him staring at her, he simply smiled back. He couldn't dart his eyes away and pretend he hadn't been sitting there mesmerized by her.

However, her mirth faltered once he spoke, "I'm pleased you accepted my mother's invitation. You shall find not much has changed."

"That is precisely what I fear." His eyebrows pulled together. "'Tis as if I've stepped back in time. Only everyone has aged and my family has vanished."

He reached his hand across the table and held hers. "I wish staying here didn't distress you."

"I know you do, and I thank you for your concern." She pulled her hand away, and whether she meant to or not, her extraction rubbed like a rebuke. "However, I cannot feign that it doesn't, and hence, you must know, I cannot remain here."

He nearly fell off his chair. "To where shall you go?"

"I know not yet. But I must pursue work." She pushed her oatmeal around in her bowl. "If I'm ever to fulfil my dream of breeding horses, I need money to purchase them and a homestead with a stable."

He dipped his chin. "But please, there's no need for haste. Thanks to me, you can no longer return home. So, I say this with heartfelt earnestness, you are most welcome to remain here in perpetuity."

She forced a smile.

That caused his jaw to clench. If being here tortured her, that pained him more than his battle wound.

*   *   *

Lachlan stood beside the carriage in wait of the women. When Fiona came into sight, he grabbed hold of a wheel. Her pink gown was the color of the sky at sunset and it exuded feminine sweetness.

She had done something different with her hair, as well. Her light brown locks now fell around her in curls. How she had fashioned it into ringlets he knew not, but he admired how it bounced as she walked to the carriage.

"Lachlan." His mother's voice came from his side and startled him. "Are you not here for the express purpose of helping *me* up?"

189

He kept his head down to avoid acknowledging the amused expression on her face, as he regained his composure and handed her up to his father, who sat holding the reins.

"You look lovely." His father complimented her, but their conversation faded as Fiona came to stand before him.

"You're staring at me." Her gaze dropped to her gown. "Is my manner of dress incorrect?" She fidgeted with the ribbon pulled tight, high above her waist. "Perhaps I ought to have borrowed one of your sisters' gowns? This dress may not be considered fashionable here." Her fingers found a ringlet of hair and she pulled it sideways. "And I confess to lacking any knowledge of whether ladies in these parts fashion their hair this way."

"I must apologize for not being able to offer you any assistance regarding the apparel, or more precisely the appearance, of other ladies, but if my opinion holds any merit, I deem you beautiful." Stunning, would have been a more precise term, seeing as she had just stolen the air from his lungs.

"Thank you for your kind words, but I am still at the mercy of my nerves." She took his hand, but he didn't help her into the carriage.

"You needn't be, I assure you. All shall be well." He squeezed her fingers. "And besides, you may rely on me for support and stay by my side the entire excursion if need be."

She smiled. "That is most sweet of you to offer, I am much obliged."

He dipped his chin, and as much as he would have fancied gazing upon her for the remainder of the day, he assisted her into the carriage.

Climbing up after her, he swallowed hard. He hadn't hesitated to offer himself as her companion for the day, but did he wish to have her by his side for the rest of his life?

They arrived without a minute to spare, and with only a nod in greeting to others, they slipped into their pew. Eyes honed in on Fiona and the congregation buzzed with whispers.

'Twas more than he thought she could bear.

He smiled at her, hoping to reassure her. She didn't smile back. If only they'd hush and set their minds to prayer. He reached over and squeezed her hand when he thought no one could see. That didn't appear to ease her tension either.

Then he saw tears well in her eyes and he knew she wasn't concerned about the townsfolk. She must be remembering her last church services, when she had attended with her family, and then observed their funerals.

He locked his fingers together to stop himself from taking her in his arms the way he had yesterday. His chest ached, as he sat beside her with no way to comfort her. Prayer was his only course of action—for now anyway.

"Lachlan." Jamilyn West stalked straight toward him and Fiona the moment they exited the church. "You never sent word that you had taken a bride." The pastor's daughter eyed her in assessment.

"Precisely. For I have not yet wed," he retorted.

A smile split Jamilyn's lips. "In that case, I shall be sure everyone knows as much." She shot Fiona a disparaging look, before she threw her arms around him. "Welcome home."

He didn't return her hug. "Thank you." He turned his head, so when she drew away from him with a kiss, her lips landed on his cheek.

Fiona's mouth gaped. Did she disapprove of how Jamilyn conducted herself or was she jealous? His eyebrow hitched, but she clamped her lips shut, and swiftly changed her demeanor. "I'm Fiona Robertson." She curtsied.

Jamilyn hesitated to respond in kind. "Fiona is an old family friend," he filled the silence. "She lived here before your family moved to New Callander."

"I see." Jamilyn's eyes narrowed, until recognition betook her. "I've heard stories about you. Your family died of Yellow Fever, and you were consequently sent to live, only God knows where, in Upper Canada. Am I correct?"

He cringed. Delicacy wasn't Jamilyn's forte.

"Aye," her voice was flat. "I returned yesterday—from Queenston."

Jamilyn's eyes darted to hers. "*Queenston*? One of my uncles conducts business there. Years ago, I visited and became acquainted with someone I now consider one of my dearest friends. We remain steadfast in our correspondence. Perhaps you're acquainted with her? Her name is Miss Penelope Sherwood."

She crossed her arms. "I believe my late aunt and her mother were bosom-friends since childhood. However, I regret that Penelope and I never had much chance to become close. I haven't spoken to her in years."

"How unfortunate. I wonder if she even remembers you?" Fiona shrugged. "I suppose it matters not, seeing as you're here now," Jamilyn mused. "I think it only best you come with me." She wouldn't be deterred, and tucked her arm into Fiona's. "I'm certain your old acquaintances shall wish to greet you, and besides, it seems Lachlan's friends wish to welcome him home."

He lost sight of her as his cousin, Blair McAllister, and best friend, Cole Munro, created a barrier as they talked.

"Please assemble behind the church, the food has been laid on the tables," Pastor West's voice rose above the crowd. "Help yourselves to dinner, and we shall see to some games afterward."

"I've been eagerly anticipating this picnic for some time now." Cole slapped Lachlan on the back with an enormous grin. "Please excuse me, for I must secure myself a seat next to Jamilyn."

"You shall require assistance." Blair nudged his cousin, Cole, in the ribs. "You always do."

"Is that so?" They spared with one another.

He shook his head with a laugh, then ambled toward where Fiona now stood with two younger lasses. "Ladies." He dipped his hat.

"You're everyone's hero, Lachlan," one of them chided. "And not simply because of your contribution to the war, but for bringing Fiona home."

"A hero?" He snickered. "I don't believe I warrant that title. But I do agree 'tis wonderful Fiona has returned."

"I'm sorry to be a contrarian, but I must adamantly argue that you are a hero," Fiona said forthright. "I cannot stomach the thought of what may have befallen me if you had not been the one sent to my homestead."

Speechless, he stared at her. She thought him a hero. Nay. That's not how he saw himself. Not now. Not with this. He moved the sling on his shoulder.

"I cannot stomach these hunger pangs any longer," one of the lasses joked. "We must partake in the dinner." She pulled her sister away. "We hope to see you both later at the games."

Fiona waved. "They've retained their sweet constitutions from childhood. I suppose some things never change."

"Not the important things." He marveled at the tiny green flecks in her hazel eyes before he remembered his manners. "Would you care for some dinner?"

"Not yet." She glanced toward the church. "Unless you do?"

"I can wait, especially now that you've piqued my curiosity. Is there something you wish to do instead?"

"Would you be so kind as to help me pick flowers?"

"If it pleases you."

She smiled. "I saw some lovely ones over yonder."

"Lead the way." He gestured with his right arm and soon they fell into step with one another. "Unfortunately, I cannot boast at my prowess for picking flowers. 'Tisn't an activity I've had much practice at." He smirked, then rubbed his chin. "Actually, I don't believe I've ever partaken in it."

"Then just as my aunt taught me, I shall teach you." She stopped. "See these. They're daisy fleabane." She picked some small flowers with white spiked petals that shot out of yellow centers. "They're pretty, are they not?"

He nodded.

"Oh, and these are pretty, as well." Her skirt swished and he strode to keep up with her as she led them to another patch where tiny orange star-shaped flowers grew in clumps the size of his fist. "These are my favorite." She picked one and smelled it with her eyes closed. "This butterfly weed grew wild behind our house. As such, they're perfect."

He followed along as she picked a bunch more, but he found himself more enthralled by her than the flowers.

"These are chicory, and these—" she held some white flowers out to him "—these are Queen Ann's lace." She laughed when he took them and held them awkwardly. "I wished you to smell them, not hold them. But if you're afraid, I assure you, there aren't any bees on them."

"I thought only to help." He arched a brow. "You wouldn't presume to think I'm afraid of bees, would you?" He stood at his full height and puffed out his chest, which caused her to laugh even more.

"Not a strapping man such as yourself." A flush crept onto her cheeks that made him smile. She turned to glance at a landing Monarch butterfly.

"Good." He winked. "And I shall take what you said in jest as a compliment."

"Of course." She reached down to pick some purple flowers.

He finally did as she bid and brought the white ones he held to his nose. "These smell like carrots."

"That's because they are. Wild ones." She ran her fingers along the roots. "If they didn't smell like carrots, they would be poison hemlock. The plant that killed Socrates."

"Good to know." He smelled them again.

"I believe we've gathered enough." She examined what she held. "I wouldn't wish to pick all the flowers."

"Until I know what they're intended for, I cannot agree or disagree with you."

"True. Then, you must trust me."
She arranged the flowers into three
equal bunches. "Can you carry this
bouquet?"

"Certainly." He took the flowers.

Her voice became devoid of
playfulness. "Now, whilst I can, I
wish to visit my family's graves. I
cannot bear to leave New Callander
without visiting them."

He nodded. However, he didn't
understand why she remained adamant
about leaving, and spoke about it in
such great measure. As far as he was
concerned, 'twasn't an urgent matter.
He had never given her a reason to
feel as if she must leave. And yet. He
couldn't give her a reason to stay.
Not with this. He shifted his arm in
the sling.

"Are you certain you're prepared
for this?"

She scrutinized her flowers.
"Nay, but I must see this through."

He dipped his chin, then led them
into the graveyard behind the church.

"If I remember correctly," she
paused. "They're buried by that tree."
And yet her head darted about. "Of

course, I may be mistaken. The trees do appear much larger now."

"The years may have passed, but some things are never forgotten." He stalked past the scatterings of tombstones. "They're here."

She pursed her lips and inhaled deeply as she set her flowers down in front of the thin rectangular stone that marked her parents' grave. He placed his down on the adjoining plot that belonged to her brother.

She knelt in between the tombstones and ran her fingers along the names and dates. From the other side of her brother's grave, he took her hand when she had finished. They prayed silently.

"Thank you for coming with me." She squeezed his fingers.

He looked at her hand. It fit perfectly in his. "I'm glad I came."

She smiled. "We ought to return to the picnic though." She relinquished his hand and rose. After pressing her fingers against her lips, she bent down to lay a kiss on each tombstone.

"I pray this affords you comfort."

She dipped her chin and hugged herself as they walked away. His right hand sought to support his left elbow to ease the ache in his shoulder. Her brows pinched with concern. "I pray you find contentment here, as well." She laid her hand on his arm. "Though I must apologize if I've turned to-day into a somber affair. This is a picnic and we do have much to be thankful for." A spark lit in her hazel eyes. "Do you fathom we may forget our troubles for one afternoon?"

She had attempted to cheer him up? He stood astonished—and immensely pleased. "I shall strive to accomplish that endeavor."

"Excellent." Her smile widened. "However, I cannot remember when I last took time to enjoy myself. I believe I've forgotten how to partake of such amusements."

"Impossible." He shook his head. "But if you require instruction, simply watch the children." A sly smile spread across his lips. "Although, it has been my experience that the oldest children delight more in their diversions." He tugged one of her curls.

"Do not revive that childhood nonsense again." She poked his chest.

"Otherwise?"

"You do not wish to know." She laughed and ran ahead several paces as they reentered the church's picnic area and strode to the tables covered with roast beef, boiled potatoes, bread, and peas.

"I dare say you're both late." Jamilyn stepped in between them once food had been piled on their plates. "Essentially everyone has finished their meals, but come with me, Fiona, and I shall secure you a pleasant place to eat."

Over her shoulder, Fiona glanced at Lachlan. He waved with a shrug. "Enjoy." She held in a sigh. She couldn't possibly have refused Jamilyn. The pastor's daughter was simply determined to welcome her back into the community.

"This should suit." Jamilyn found space on a blanket spread over a patch of grass beneath a broad maple tree.

"Shall you not sit with me?" she asked once she had sat in the shade with her skirt tucked in properly.

"I've already eaten. And besides, I must ensure everyone enjoys themselves."

She nodded. "Duties must abound for a pastor's daughter."

"Aye, they most certainly do." Jamilyn peered down at her. "But before I take my leave, may I inquire as to the length of your stay."

"You most certainly may. However, I cannot answer definitively." She speared a potato whilst Jamilyn stared at her questionably. "It hinges on the speed in which I can secure work."

The lass' eyebrows shot up. "Perhaps I may be of some assistance." She dropped next to her.

"I would be much obliged." She shifted to allow plenty of room on the plaid woolen blanket. "I had been diligently working toward becoming a breeder of quarter horses. Now however—" her voice trailed off.

But, the dark-haired lass overtook the conversation in earnest, "Are you willing to move from New Callander?"

She hesitated, then nodded.

"Fabulous. I have an uncle in Boston that may be in need of someone. I shall send word to him posthaste."

"Thank you." She prayed God would lead her where she was meant to be.

"'Tis truly my pleasure." Jamilyn beamed as she stood. She followed the woman's gaze as it roamed over the other guests and rested on Lachlan.

"Is that Mr. and Mrs. Munro with Lachlan?" She bounded to her feet.

"Aye."

"Thank you for your trouble in securing me such a beautiful place to eat, but I must greet them." She didn't allow Jamilyn time to interject, as she strode past a sea of Queen Ann's Lace.

"Fiona." Mrs. Munro pulled her into an embrace that would have knocked her plate to the ground had Lachlan not grabbed it.

"Mrs. Munro." She looked into her kind face. "How good to see you."

"And you, as well, sweet lass."
They held each other's hands. "My, my,
look at the beautiful woman you've
become." She twisted her hand about,
and a look of concern etched her
wrinkles. "But how is it that there is
no ring on your finger? Have all the
young lads gone daft?" She grimaced at
Lachlan. "Are you in need of some
spectacles?"

Her cheeks flamed red. She didn't
dare look at him.

"Cait, you're embarrassing them."
Mr. Munro shook his head. "Poor
Lachlan is about to perspire
profusely."

"My dear, Finnean." Cait shook
her head. "If it has escaped your
notice, let me remind you, I'm an
elderly woman now. And as such, I'm
prone to some idiosyncrasies, which I
believe are granted to those who have
lived as long as I have." She laughed
and they all laughed with her. She
couldn't begrudge Cait anything. She
was, and had always been, a woman with
the kindest of hearts.

"I'm glad to see you well."
Finnean shook her hand in the most

welcoming way and she returned his sentiment.

"I was just speaking to them about your desire to breed Quarter Horses." Lachlan handed her plate back to her.

"You must call on us, Fiona," Finnean offered. "You were good with horses when you were younger and I shall welcome an opportunity to observe what you've learned since then."

"Thank you," she couldn't suppress her joy. "I'd be delighted to accept your invitation."

"Wonderful. Call on us whenever 'tis convenient for you." Finnean smiled at her and she nodded.

"And whenever that is, you must come in so we may lengthen our chat," Cait added. "If you wish, you may even bring Lachlan." She winked at him. "We shall all share a meal."

"Thank you," she laughed with a glance at Lachlan.

"Wonderful." Cait's smile turned to Lachlan. "Your grandparents are eager to welcome you home. However, they volunteered to supervise the children playing at the waterfall."

"You ought to surprise them," Finnean grinned. "They shall be ecstatic to see you."

"I ought to have known where to find my grandparents," Lachlan chuckled. "They've always had an attachment to waterfalls."

"Aye," Finnean agreed. "These falls remind them of Bracklinn Falls, where they grew up."

Cait's expression turned wistful, "There's was a true young love."

"Not just young," Finnean countered. "They're just as much in love to-day, as they were when they lived in Scotland."

"We all ought to be so fortunate." Cait put her hands together as if in prayer.

"We are." Finnean put his arm around her.

"Oh, stop." She swatted his chest, but Fiona saw the love and admiration in her eyes as clear as water.

"I do believe 'tis you who is now embarrassed," Lachlan taunted Cait.

She pointed her finger at him.
"Go see your grandparents."

He nodded with a grin. "Care to
join me, Fiona?"

"Certainly." They bid them
farewell, then enjoyed their dinner as
they strolled to the waterfall.

"Seanair, Seanmhair," Lachlan
called to his grandparents in Scots'
Gaelic.

Almost knee deep in water, Sheena
and Logan waved. They left the
responsibility of watching the young
children to a group of adolescent
girls, before they waddled, hand in
hand, to dry land.

"Lachlan." His grandmother held
him close. "Your parents warned us you
were injured. Please, tell us your
wound is healing?"

"It improves every day." He
patted his shoulder.

"Hear, hear!" His grandfather
embraced him.

"And this lovely lass can only be
Fiona." Lachlan's grandmother hugged
her. "Welcome home, dear."

"Thank you." She swallowed the
lump in her throat—*home*? New

Callander hadn't been her *home* for eighteen years.

"Aye, welcome home." Lachlan's grandfather bowed. "We were informed by Maisie and Ennis that you saved our Lachlan."

Her eyes darted to Lachlan. Last night, after she had retired, he must have told his parents what she had done. What *he knew* she had done, since she hadn't disclosed the entire narrative about her dealings with Doctor Blackstone.

"We owe you a debt of gratitude," Logan continued.

"Nay." She shook her head. "I'm just thankful I was able to help."

Sheena and Logan shared a knowing look. Did they believe her and Lachlan to be in love? She averted her gaze to the waterfall. They were friends. And friends didn't simply remain idle whilst one of them faced death.

"You were courageous," Sheena said. "You both have shown tremendous heroism."

Now it was Lachlan who shook his head, unable to accept the compliment. But his grandmother wouldn't be deterred. "We wish to hold a celebration in honor of you both. At our home, on Saturday."

"That's most kind, but not necessary." Lachlan looked between his grandparents.

"A homecoming party, then? You shan't possibly object to that," Sheena insisted, and looked to her husband for support.

"I'm beginning to suspect your questions are rhetorical." Lachlan rubbed his brow.

"Your grandmother has always possessed a strong sense of duty." Logan smiled into his wife's shining amber eyes. "Best not to impede her—unless absolutely necessary."

Some remembrance passed between them, before Sheena turned her smile from Logan onto them. "Don't fret, I shall be by tomorrow to discuss it further. Now go, enjoy this lovely day God gave us." She grabbed her husband's hand. "We have a waterfall we promised to supervise."

As they waded back into the

water, they waved goodbye. "I've always revered my grandparents." He broke their silence.

"I can understand why." She watched them laugh as they lovingly splashed each other. She hadn't played with such inhibition since she was a wee lass.

"I thought we agreed to enjoy ourselves to-day?" He shook his head in disgust. "If we continue to simply observe others, we shall certainly fail."

"We shall not fail," she emphasized each word. "We must remedy this poste haste."

He couldn't suppress a grin. "What do you propose?"

*F*iona stopped. "For someone who's supposed to be enjoying himself, you have a rather serious look upon your face."

"I apologize." Lachlan offered his hand and helped her climb over a fallen tree trunk. "Being in the woods

reminds me of my last march with my
regiment." He looked up through the
trees, to where a ray of sunshine had
broken through. "I can hear the war
cries, smell the musket smoke, see my
soldiers fall—" his hand went to his
shoulder "—I thought I would die."

"Oh, Lachlan," she grimaced. "How
foolish of me to suggest a walk
through the woods. I'm truly sorry, I
ought to have known. Let's go back."
She turned, but he didn't help her
back over the rotten timber.

"Don't apologize. How could you
have known when I myself did not?" He
raked his fingers through his hair.
"May I ask you something?"

She nodded. "Anything."

His voice was barely audible, "So
many men were killed in that battle,
why was I spared?"

She grasped his hand. "That
question has plagued me my entire
life. Why did I not die of Yellow
Fever? Why was I not trapped in that
burning barn?" She glimpsed at the
past, then her eyes struck his. "I
believe it to be God's will. He wants
you here, Lachlan."

"Do you suppose we shall ever learn why?"

She shrugged. "I pray we do."

"As do I." He nodded. "But in the meantime, I shall continue to thank Him for placing you in my life." He rubbed his thumb over the soft skin of her hand.

Her lips curved in the most pleasing manner. "We are of the same mind." She stepped to the other side of the fallen chestnut tree and he followed her. "I cannot count the number of times I've thanked God for sending you to my homestead."

"Why would you thank Him for that?" He released her hand. "Before my regiment captured your homestead, you were close to fulfilling your dream. Now here you are, in another country, far from achieving your goal."

Her face rumpled with serious deliberation. "When you pose it that way—" She couldn't remain disdainful any longer and laughed as she sat on the log and peered up at him. "You cannot dispute the protection and support you offered me. Without you, I shudder to think what may have transpired."

"That's precisely what I fail to understand." He sat next to her, and as much as the words lacerated his tongue they needed to be spoken. "I heard the doctor talk about marrying you." Her eyebrows slammed together. "As your affianced, ought not he have been able to offer you his protection, or at least support?"

"When, or how, did you hear that Edgar and I were to be married?"

"The day before I marched out to battle, he came to visit, and I heard him mutter something about what would become of your dog once you were married."

"You misunderstood him."

Misunderstood? He tried, but couldn't decipher a different meaning.

"Edgar and I were never betrothed." She wrung her hands as she rose.

He jumped to his feet. "You weren't?"

"Nay." She shivered with disgust, her face pursed as if she had drank soured milk. "I've never loved him."

She began to walk along the path that led out of the woods.

"Then why did he discuss marriage?"

She rolled her eyes. "He's talked about marriage since my aunt and uncle died."

He kicked a rock. It scuttled along the earthen floor and landed under a clump of poison ivy. "Am I to assume then, that he loved you, and when you didn't return his love, he became embittered?"

"Nay," she sneered. "We both hold a mutual dislike for one another."

"Fiona." He halted her at the edge of the woods. "I fail to understand."

"'Tis unimportant now." She stepped out of the woods into the sunlight.

"I disagree." He followed her and she slowed her pace. He must know what she attempted to keep from him. And why?

"Lachlan, I foolishly misjudged Edgar. I believed him, and put my trust in him, but he possesses the most vengeful heart."

"What did you trust him with?" He stepped in closer to her and took hold of her shoulder. "Me?" She didn't meet his eyes and looked over his right hand as she nodded. "Please, confide in me." Her head whipped back. She stared at him. Uncertainty clouded her eyes. "Please, Fiona," he tenderly beseeched her.

"Fine." Her shoulders slumped and he drew his hand down to his side. "I believe Edgar's cousin, Mrs. Johnson, spread rumors around Queenston about my virtue. She misconstrued my being alone with a regiment of American soldiers. And whether she did Edgar's bidding, or he merely took advantage of her lies, I shall never know. But he was adamant that, should I wish to save my reputation, I could only do so by becoming his wife."

Anger forged within him. How loathsome! To trick someone into marriage!

"Nevertheless, I infuriated him by refusing his proposal." She rubbed her neck, and he prayed the doctor had not hurt her. "But then I found you injured, and you needed medical attention. Edgar was nearby, and known far and wide as one of the best surgeons in Upper Canada."

His hands fisted. His jaw clenched.

"At first, I thought I would have to marry him to obtain his willingness to help."

His eyes grew large. *Impossible. She shan't have.*

"However, Edgar only wished to marry me as a means of obtaining my land."

"Your land?"

"Aye." She took a deep breath. "Before my aunt married his uncle, Edgar was to inherit the property. But my uncle loved me as a daughter and bequeathed his land to me."

"The doctor was your uncle's nephew?" She nodded, her lips pursed. "Continue. Please, Fiona."

She twirled a ringlet of her corn silk hair. "He left me no other choice. I had to agree to his terms. I couldn't allow you to die."

His body went rigid. "What terms?" he ground out.

"Edgar agreed to tend to you—"
She bit her lip.

"If?" he urged, although he
wasn't certain he could bear to hear
what she'd tell him.

"If I relinquished my homestead
with nearly all my possessions."

He stared at her, unable to
breathe. His body numbed. "Nay," he
murmured. She had lost everything to
save him. "I cannot express how sorry
I am."

"Don't apologize," she held firm.
"I shan't ever regret what I did. And
I dare say, your family would agree I
chose wisely." She glanced at the
picnic festivities. "Your brethren
love you." She hugged herself. "Your
grandparents even wish to throw a
party in your honor."

"It ought to be entirely in *your*
honor."

"Nay." She turned on him.
"Please, promise me you shan't allow
that. I merely did what I had to do.
And I shan't wish for my dealings with
Edgar to be public knowledge. I long
to forget how badly my reputation was
tarnished."

"But your sacrifice was too great. I shall never be able to repay you."

She glared at him. "Life isn't about repayment. You don't owe me anything. I'm happy knowing I did what was required of me, what God wanted from me."

Wide-eyed, he stared at her. He couldn't believe all she had done to help him. His childhood thoughts of how wonderful she was, failed to even come close to how amazing he knew her to be now.

"I still don't understand something."

"What?" Her voice softened.

"Why did the doctor chase after us if you gave him what he asked for?"

"Either he reneged on our agreement, or he didn't appreciate that I took his horse."

"*His horse*?" He rubbed the back of his neck. "I thought Hope belonged to you?"

"She did. But Edgar claimed the horse lived off the land, and as such was tied to the land, and thus his."

"So he thought *you* broke your agreement."

"But I didn't. I left him a note stating that I was merely borrowing Hope. I had every intention of returning the horse to him," she spoke most emphatically, then shrugged. "Perhaps Edgar didn't find my note, or if he did, perhaps he didn't read it in its entirety, or he merely didn't believe me."

He wished to punch something. She had sacrificed her life for him. She had lost her home, all her possessions, her dreams for the future. She had been close to breeding horses, but now she must begin anew. And all this for him. "You must rue the day I walked back into your life, for I've done nothing but destroy it."

Her mouth gaped.

"There you are." Jamilyn startled them. "And both looking positively morose for a picnic." She tutted. "Come, Fiona." The pastor's daughter took her arm. However, she remained unmovable, her eyes locked with his. "Please," Jamilyn said through gritted teeth. "I wish to see how well you fare in our games." With force, she tugged her away.

He stared after her with utter astonishment. She had sacrificed everything to save him. She may not wish his recompense, but with God's help, he would repay her.

*   *   *

Yesterday had thoroughly tired Fiona. Her emotions had been spent with Lachlan, and then Jamilyn kept her body in movement with one game after another—hoop rolling, stilt walking, checkers, dominoes—the list went on and on, for the pastor's daughter had made it her vocation to enlist her in nearly every diversion.

Hence, she didn't see Lachlan again until they had climbed into the carriage to travel home. And by then, she had to summon all her fortitude to force her eyelids to remain open. Intelligible conversation hadn't been possible.

"Good morning." Lachlan rose and offered her a chair as she entered the kitchen.

"Good morning." She sat at the wooden table. "Thank you." He returned to his seat opposite her. "Are your parents not joining us?"

"They're performing their morning chores." He sipped his drink.

"Shall I help them?" She flattened her hands on the smooth table about to push herself up.

"Nay." He set his cup down and poured her tea. "They imparted strict instructions unto me that I shan't allow their guest to work. And I'm not much use." He shrugged and pain clouded his eyes. "I must remember not to move my shoulder." His hand fisted until the torment subsided. "Pardon me, I hoped you would consent to join me to-day? I wish to show you some things."

"Oh?" Her mind raced with interest.

"Only if you wish." He stood and set about assembling her breakfast. "Please, don't feel obliged."

"Nay, nay. I welcome the amusement." She met his uncertain eyes, as he placed a plate before her. "I'm certain it shall be fun." She squinted at him. "It *shall* be fun, shall it not?" He laughed. "Care to tell me where I may anticipate going?"

He shook his brown locks. "You've already consented without knowing the particulars. Now, you shall just have to wait and see." He winked.

"Fine." She tried to look perturbed, but how could she against that charming smile. "I hope you haven't gone to much trouble?"

"Nay, none at all." The brown of his eyes held an enigmatic glint. She fought hard to look down at her food.

"Thank you." She cracked the hardboiled egg before her. "I cannot wait to set off."

"Nor I." He popped the last bit of his egg into his mouth and swallowed it with a mischievous grin.

"Are we to travel far?" Fiona eyed the McAllister carriage as they neared it.

"Nay, but I thought it best to conserve our energy."

"Whatever for?" She squinted at him, but Lachlan didn't reveal any

clues. "You are very mysterious to-
day."

He laughed. "I wished to be more
so, but I fear I must ask you to
drive." He motioned to his shoulder.

"Certainly." She accepted his
hand as he helped her into the
carriage.

After he walked around the horses
and climbed up beside her, she asked,
"How is your injury?"

"Better every hour. I believe
'tis healing. The wound hasn't
reopened. Although, I wish 'twould
heal quicker. Waiting is its own form
of torture."

She nodded. She fully understood
his sentiment. Waiting to make her
living breeding horses, was certainly
providing her a good lesson in
patience.

She held the reins tight in her
hands. "Which way shall I direct the
horses?"

"That way." He pointed, then
settled back in his seat.

She was about to issue a command
when his direction seized her. "If we

go that way, we shall pass directly by my family's old homestead."

"Precisely." She didn't know what she had expected, but this was most certainly not it. She sat petrified as she listened to him. "However, I never intended to *pass* by it. I thought you'd prefer to go in it." The leather dug into her hands. "But if I was mistaken—" Concern etched his features.

She eased her grip on the reins. "Nay, this is a lovely surprise. It shall do me good." She verbally reconciled herself to their destination. Hopefully her heart and her mind would follow. "I've already come this far, and I did see it the other day—"

"If you'd rather not—"

"Nay. We shall go." She commanded the horses to start their journey, then prayed for strength. "It appears unchanged." She stopped the carriage in front of the one and a half storey house and stared at the stone structure. The wooden door and paned windows showed no sign of decay. The sloped tile roof was in good repair.

The chimneys and walls arose with a sturdiness thanks to the different size bricks her ancestors had labored to fit together like quilts made of rock. "I see no one about. Does no one live here?"

"Nay, the owner lives elsewhere and endeavors to sell this homestead?" She sat stunned, as he descended the carriage and walked around the horses before he offered her his hand to help her down.

"What has the asking price been set at?" She admired the vegetation as he led her to the front door.

"I know not." He produced a key and unlocked the door. "Shall I inquire on your behalf?" He eyed her.

"Nay, I don't believe I would be able to afford it. And even if I could, living here would render me unable to work elsewhere, and I desperately need to earn more money to purchase a breeding pair of Quarter Horses?" He dipped his chin, then stepped aside so she could enter ahead of him.

The air was stale and heavy, no doubt from the house being closed during this exceedingly warm weather. Gone were the scents of her mother's cooking and the cheerfulness of her father's whistling. However, it appeared essentially as she remembered it.

Upon entering the front door, a staircase rose immediately before them. On her left was the parlor, and on her right, the sitting room. She looked in both rooms. There were some new decorations and furnishings, but most of her family's furniture remained.

Back in the wee vestibule, she walked along the narrow passageway, beside the stairs, to the kitchen at the back of the house. Her eyes soaked in her surroundings as she ran her hand over the knotty wooden kitchen table.

They didn't speak. He simply followed her from room to room and never encroached on her space or thoughts, but stayed close enough that his presence comforted her.

"That step still creaks." She forced a smile, as they ascended the stairs. "I imagine there is not a man

alive who could fix that. Then again,
I shan't wish anyone to try."

There were three bedrooms
upstairs, but the one that drew her in
was her former room. Memories flooded
her. She remembered her parents
tucking her into bed. Her brother
shouting goodnight to her from his
room.

She wrapped her arms around
herself. Her family's love surrounded
her. But she shan't cry she told
herself firmly. Her family had loved
her, and she them, and she'd carry
that love in her heart always, no
matter where life brought her.

*Thank you, God, for the wonderful
years I was fortunate enough to have
with my family.*

Tears pricked her eyes and she
fled the room as if she could outrun
her emotions. Her hand slid along the
banister her brother had convinced her
was safe to slide down. Oh, how her
mother had scolded them. She grinned
as she walked out the front door into
the sunshine.

After a deep breath, she turned to him. "Thank you for bringing me here."

He studied her, as if to verify that she was well before he answered. "'Twas my pleasure." He locked the door. "Are you still inclined to trust me with the itinerary for the second half of our day?"

"There's more?" she blurted.

"Aye." He grinned. "I believe I know what shall bring you happiness."

"You do?" she chuckled. "Then you must realize there is only one way to find out? You must tell me your plans."

"You present a valid argument." He walked toward the carriage.

"Lachlan." She planted her feet.

"Fine." He turned his smile upon her. "We are to dine with Finnean and Cait, and then you may spend the rest of the day with their horses."

A squeal escaped her lips. "How wonderful." She clasped her hands together in sheer delight. "You must have risen early to arrange all this."

"On the contrary, I arranged this yesterday at the picnic, whilst you competed in *all* those games."

She puffed up her cheeks with air and let out a slow, playful breath. "There were plenty, were there not?"

"Aye, and I enjoyed watching every one." He returned her smile.

Her heart quickened. She gave a nod, then began to walk back toward the carriage so he couldn't see the thoughts clearly written across her face. Had he been admiring her yesterday?

Her stomach clenched. Nay. He must be enamored with Jamilyn who had accompanied her in every game. The pastor's daughter was exceedingly pretty, and she had been the one here in New Callander with him, not her. They must have spent time together, made ample memories, fallen in love.

He certainly didn't love her in that way. He merely felt obliged to her, pitied her, and harboured a desire to repay her. Once he felt his debt was cleared he'd be free to begin his life with Jamilyn as if none of this had ever happened.

*　　*　　*

"Good morning, Fiona." Lachlan's mother greeted her as she entered the kitchen for breakfast. "Did you sleep comfortably?"

"Aye." She sat and poured herself a cup of tea. She hadn't lied. Her bed was comfortable. However, the amount of sleep she achieved was dubious. She hadn't been able to cease the multitude of thoughts that had rambled through her mind. But she would not ponder such irritants now. "I enjoyed a wonderful day yesterday."

"Shall you return to Finnean and Cait's to-day?"

"Not if I may be of any help to you."

"'Tis settled then," Maisie grinned. "Please send our warmest regards to the Munros." She placed a log on the fire. "My mother-in-law visited yesterday whilst you and Lachlan were out."

"Oh?" that solitary utterance was all she could muster.

"She delighted in discussing plans for a welcome home party." Maisie poked at the timber. It crackled in protest, much as her mind had. Saturday would mark her one week anniversary in New Callander, and as such, the celebration must be one of farewell. She needed to leave, to find work, and forge a new life for herself. When would Jamilyn hear news pertaining to that post in Boston?

"She's invited the entire town to their home on Saturday," Maisie interrupted her thoughts.

The entire town? She clutched her teacup. They were certainly proud of Lachlan and happy to have him home.

"Do you suppose you could help me cook for the celebration later this week?"

"Certainly." She stirred her tea.

"Wonderful. I'm already anticipating our time together." Her warm, compassionate face smiled down. "Good morning, Lachlan." His mother spotted him before she did.

"Good morning." He greeted them before he sat in the chair opposite her.

"Now that you've acquired other company, I shan't feel as if I'm abandoning you." Maisie removed her apron. "I do apologize for leaving, but I must feed those chickens before they attack one another."

She grinned. She hadn't been alone for any length of time since she had arrived, except whilst she was supposed to be asleep. And 'twas all in most contrary to the solitary life she had lived on her homestead in Upper Canada. There, days often passed without the sight of another person, especially during the long winter months. Her preference for this daily interaction was growing.

But her chest tightened. She had to leave. Her reasons were valid and pressing. She must brave the torment of missing Lachlan, his family, and this whole town. However, she'd do so willingly, because if life had taught her anything, 'twas that nothing ever remained the same. She'd simply enjoy each day here and then move on. No sense hoping for something that could never be.

"Are you bound for Finnean and Cait's?" he asked when the door shut behind his mother.

"'Twas my hope." She eyed him. "Shall you accompany me?"

He shook his head, then took a drink from his cup. "I have business to tend to. However, perhaps it shall cease in time for me to see you home later?"

"I'd like that." She wished to inquire into his business matter, but refused to be impertinent. If he had wished to confide in her, he would have. Besides, who was she to him? A friend? A mere house guest? A woman from his past that would soon leave, and hence, never be part of his future?

*   *   *

"Did you enjoy another fine day?" Lachlan asked Fiona, as they walked toward his carriage.

Her hazel eyes were large with enthusiasm. "A tremendous one." He smiled, for he had known before she had even answered. She simply beamed. She truly adored horses.

"Your appearance suggests you may have been thrown in the dirt though."

She laughed, and shook some dust from her brown work gown. "Not precisely. However, as is usual when one works with equine I have become a mite untidy."

His heart raced as an idea shot into his mind. "Would you care for a swim in the pond before supper?"

"How refreshing." A sparkle lit her eyes, but dulled when they rested on his shoulder. "I haven't a change of clothing."

"Neither do I. However, I would be happy to wade in up to my waist." His shoulder still bothered him, but he endeavored not to allow his sling to impede every aspect of his life. "That is, as long as you promise not to splash me."

"I could take pity on you and promise that," she cooed playfully.

"You *could* promise?" He quirked an eyebrow.

"It matters not—" her eyes peered downward "—for we still have the issue of my clothing."

"You never allowed that to affect your decisions before." He winked. "And those clothes do need a wash."

She laughed. "In this weather, I expect I would dry in the carriage before we even reached home."

He grinned. "Your words reek of acceptance."

"I have dreamed of swimming in that pond."

"Then let us make those dreams come true."

12

"Is this how you remembered the pond in your dreams?" Lachlan asked, as he and Fiona walked down a trodden path flanked with lush greenery.

"Aye, but this is better, because 'tis real." She discarded her black shoes. "Do you suppose others would regard this as foolish?"

"Foolish? Nay. Childish? Perhaps. However, the question is immaterial given that there's no one here to render judgement. And even if there were, we could throw them in and then they would agree there's nothing more refreshing or fun."

"In that case." She dipped her toes into the water's edge. "A little cool, but we shall acclimate." She dove in.

He turned to avoid having the water splash his shoulder. "What of your promise not to wet me?"

"I promised no such thing." She grinned as her hands sleeked back hair that dripped water in every direction. "I believe I said *I could take pity on you*. However, you do not seem the sort who welcomes pity." With a laugh, she sent another cascade of water toward his legs. "There. Now you're thoroughly wet, you may as well come in." Her arms moved in circles to keep her afloat. "Why must you always persist in being the last one in?"

His eyebrow hitched. She had remembered that from their childhood. But before he could reply with some witty retort, she flung herself backward with a blissful sigh.

He sauntered into the water. The soft ground beneath him suctioned his feet. He skimmed the rippling water with his right hand as he submerged himself up to his waist. She had dove under several times and was well on her way to becoming an honorary fish.

"I never allowed myself to dwell on how much I missed this pond." She swam to him. The water reflected the sun around her and she appeared as a vision.

He dipped his chin. His tongue tied. He had missed *her* being here.

She smiled. Then, barely created a wave when she swam away. His eyes refused to part with her. But he blew out a sharp breath and turned. He needed dry land. His leg muscles pushed the water aside as he ploughed through it.

He strode up the bank. If he didn't guard his heart he would become the same love smitten youth he had buried away eighteen years ago.

She hadn't once admitted to any amorous feelings for him. All she desired, was to leave.

His stomach knotted. Like a cannon that shot repeatedly, she tore at the palisade around his heart. He had to build up his armor to defend himself.

He shook his head as he fetched them each a blanket for the ride home. But he needed more than this woolen shield wrapped around himself to keep his heart intact.

*   *   *

Cooking with Lachlan's mother was anything but work. They had prepared food all day yesterday, and to-day they had already made nearly all they had planned—and 'twas scarcely past noon.

"Lachlan, get away." His mother charged at him. "Those are for Saturday's party." Fiona laughed, as he stole a wee loaf of bread and earned himself a swat from his mother's towel.

"You both can certainly cook." He eyed the mound of food laid on the table.

Maisie shook a finger at him. "Since you've nominated yourself *taste master*, is the bread to your liking?"

He labored over his last bite. "I cannot be certain." He glanced at her and a smile threatened to creep across his serious face. "I believe I shall require another loaf before I can—"

"Out!" His mother shooed him toward the door.

With a laugh, he stalled in the entranceway. "Perhaps you could spare Fiona this afternoon? After all, she is the reason I ventured into the kitchen in the first place."

Maisie eyed him, and so did she. She didn't recall having made plans.

"Of course." His mother's face brightened as she turned to her. "Go enjoy yourself. You've been cooped up in this kitchen far too long."

"Are you sure?" she asked warily.

"Aye. It shan't take me but a moment longer to finish, and we can complete the last of the cooking tomorrow."

She hesitated.

Maisie fisted a hand on her hip. "Must I shoo you out as well?"

She shook her head with a smile and kissed the sweet matron on her cheek. "I daresay you are much too kind."

"Oh, hush." Maisie held so much love in her eyes. "Shall I expect you for supper?"

"Aye, Mama." He snatched another wee loaf of bread and darted out the door.

She laughed and took off her apron, whilst his mother shook her wooden spoon in the air. "I know not what to do with that lad, perhaps a good wife shall mend his ways."

"I'm certain there are plenty of women in New Callander vying for that job." With a chuckle, she hung her apron on a peg.

But Maisie didn't laugh. "As far as I know, my son hasn't expressed an interest in anyone from town."

She fell silent. Perhaps his mother was unaware of Jamilyn?

"My thoughts pertained to you, Fiona."

"Me?" Her fingers flew to her heart.

"Aye, my dear." The other woman remained calm, which stood in sharp contrast to her.

"But, I may leave town shortly," she stammered.

"Then, perhaps you ought to reconsider."

A heat rose to her cheeks. She couldn't articulate a thought, let alone form a coherent sentence. She ironed out a wrinkle in her skirt. Anything to avoid his mother's gaze. Maisie must be mistaken. If he wished to marry her, she would know. He had never been one to hide his feelings for her—when he'd had them. She had to reiterate that point to herself. He was no longer in love with her. He was merely grateful that she had saved his life.

"I apologize if I've embarrassed you." Maisie's voice broke her reverie. "But a mother knows these things." She simply stared at her, which brought a smile to the woman's face. "I beg your pardon for speaking with such forthrightness. However, I shan't recant. After you spend the afternoon with my son perhaps you shall come to see the possibilities as I do."

She nodded. Although, 'twas not as a sign of agreement, she merely needed to distance herself from his mother and her opinions.

"Your mother and I constantly joked about the two of you."

"My mother?" her mind raced even faster than she spat her words.

"Aye, we enjoyed musing that if Lachlan and you married we would truly be family."

"But, that was merely jesting?" she shrugged off the implication.

"Perhaps not so much as hoping." Maisie's eyes shined.

"I see," she murmured and stumbled toward the door. Her head spun. "Please, excuse me." She slunk out of the kitchen. Her own mother wished her to wed Lachlan.

"You appear deep in thought." She jumped at Lachlan's voice. "Forgive my intrusion." He regarded her with concern. And she imagined she looked akin to how she felt—like a frightened horse about to bolt.

"I'm fine." Her eyes enveloped him. *Lachlan, her husband?*

"Fiona, you're staring at me." He straightened.

"Excuse me." She shook her head and lumbered a few feet away to rest her gaze on anything but him.

He snickered as he came to her side. "Whatever could have happened from the time I left the kitchen until now?"

Her eyes flew to his. She studied their brown depths, as if they held the answers she sought.

"Did my mama say something to upset you?"

"Nay, your mother's been nothing but lovely." She needed to drown these thoughts until later. Alone in her bedroom, she could spend another sleepless night sifting through them. But not here and not now. She must hide her uncertainty and turmoil.

"Please accept my apology if I've worried you unnecessarily." She pasted on a smile. But the lift of his brow told her he was unconvinced. "Perhaps you would be so kind as to divulge the reason why you invited me out with you this afternoon?" The question was supposed to steer their attention in another direction, and yet, it made her heart quicken. Why had he sought her company?

A gleam lightened his eyes and his features softened. "I craved your insight, and dared to hope you would help me tend to someone special."

A jolt of jealousy struck her. "*Someone special?*" She clasped her hands in front of her stomach and rubbed one thumb over the other. However, it did not soothe her.

"Aye, she certainly is special." He pulled her arm until her fingers unclenched. Then he took hold of them. His warm hand, big and strong, fit flawlessly in hers. "Come. You must meet the newest lass in my life."

She faltered. Could she do this? "I don't believe I—"

"Please. She arrived this morning, and you're the only person I've longed to introduce her to." He pulled gently, and she followed him across the farm. A smile settled on his face. She ought to be happy for him. He had this other lass who obviously filled him with joy.

"I hope you find her agreeable." He stood in front of her, and she couldn't see anything beyond him.

"Actually," she murmured. "I know not if I—"

"Please." He squeezed her hand. "This is of great importance to me. I require nothing less than your honest opinion of her."

Since when, had her opinion on whom he should love matter?

"I wish you could have accompanied me to see her before I handed over my money. But, alas, that option wasn't at my disposal."

Was he referring to some sort of dowry? *God, why am I here?*

"She truly is a beauty."

Her heart sank. But she forced her lips to curl up. He was in love with this other lass. She must be glad for them. "I'm certain that if you love her, I shall love her, as well."

"Splendid." He stepped aside and pointed out into the distant pasture. A sleek brown figure frolicked in the sun. "There she is."

"A horse?" Her eyes bulged. "You purchased a horse?"

"Not just any horse. A Quarter Horse mare. Lovely, is she not?"

She swallowed hard before she attempted to speak. "She's gorgeous."

"Do you wish to ride her? I haven't had the privilege." He tipped his head toward his bandaged shoulder. "And I would greatly esteem your opinion of her."

"I'd be honored." She demurred, and trailed his jovial gait to the stable. She needed this ride to steady her nerves. To put some distance between them. To eradicate any thought of him, before she did or said something she might regret later.

*   *   *

"Lachlan." Jamilyn waved at him from atop her carriage. He raised a hand in greeting and strode forward to help her down.

This was an unexpected visit. What had necessitated her to make such a trip when they'd meet tomorrow at the party?

"You appear in good health." Her eyes travelled the length of him. "I hope your injury is healing much faster now that you're home."

"It has been improving daily." He thanked her. "Are you well?"

"Very well, indeed." Her smile grew. "I've come with news for Fiona."

"She's indoors with my mama. They're cooking for tomorrow's party."

"I'm eagerly anticipating that event." She clapped. "I hope you shall save a dance, or two, or more, for me?" She giggled. "I do love to dance a quadrille."

He dipped his chin. To outright refuse would have been rude.

"You know I fancy nothing more than to remain here and speak with you, but this news is burning my tongue, I must part with it." She laid a hand on his forearm. Her voice softened, "Although, perhaps afterward we could speak more?"

"A fine suggestion." He patted her hand amicably. "However, I regret that I must decline. I have work."

"Another time then." She stepped in closer to him. "Perhaps tomorrow night. We can spend the entire evening together."

He shifted his weight—away from her. Cole had always been smitten with Jamilyn, and he would do whatever he could to steer her affections toward his friend. "I'm certain there shall be plenty of agreeable men forced to duel if you do not grant them the opportunity of a dance with you." He looked toward the house as she trilled a response he couldn't decipher. "But please, don't allow me to keep you any longer than necessary. I shall take you to Fiona."

"Wonderful." She slid her hand farther up into the crevice of his arm.

He drew his lips into a tight smile and led her past the kitchen window. Fiona and his mother looked out. Jamilyn pressed herself in closer to him as she waved.

The women returned her salutation. Although they didn't smile. Then Fiona disappeared from view. Had she been jealous? Nay. For her to be bothered by another woman on his arm, she would have to harbor feelings for him.

He peered down at the gravel path that crunched under their feet. Most likely they knew of Jamilyn's news and didn't wish to hear it. Curiosity vigorously entwined itself around him. "After you." He held the door open.

"Thank you." She smiled and hesitated before she released his arm.

"Jamilyn, to what do we owe this honor?" His mother bustled out of the kitchen.

"Mrs. McAllister," Jamilyn greeted her. "I've come to see Fiona."

"How considerate of you." His mother kept a smile firmly planted on her lips. "Lachlan, do see if Fiona has finished in the kitchen. I shall be with Jamilyn in the drawing room." She turned to the pastor's daughter.

"I do wish to inquire after your father."

"Sure, Mama." He went into the kitchen. "Fiona?" She stood with her back to him. Could she not face him? He slowly approached her. "Jamilyn has come to visit with you."

"I shall go directly," she grunted over her shoulder. "But first, I must—move—these—out of here—before they burn." She studied the biscuits she had wrestled from the fire. "Do you suppose they're eatable?"

"Only one way to ascertain that." He plucked one from the table, and blew on it, before he sank his teeth into the warm treat. "Delicious. As always."

She fiddled with this one and that. "Another minute or two and I dare say they would have been ruined."

"Then you saved them just in the nick of time." He popped the remainder in his mouth. "Precisely as you saved me." He smiled.

However, she remained pensive and didn't look at him. "I had better hurry. I've kept Jamilyn waiting far too long." She untied her apron, pulled it over her head, and untangled it from her light brown hair.

"I shall hang that for you." He reached for the apron and she stilled when their hands met.

"Thank you," she mumbled with the drop of her hand, then quickly backed out of the room, obviously distressed—and that was even more so than yesterday when he had showed her the mare. Her peculiar behavior must pertain to Jamilyn. But why? He threw the apron on a peg and strode to the drawing room to find out.

"The tea must have steeped by now," his mother excused herself as he entered.

"Lachlan." Jamilyn sat on their sand-colored sofa, across from Fiona, who was perched on a padded chair. "Sit next to me." She patted the cushion. He dipped his chin, and went to her side. Irritated that again he couldn't refuse her request.

With tight lips, Fiona smiled. "Jamilyn was about to divulge her news."

He looked from her pained expression to Jamilyn's amused face.

"Aye, and such wonderful news."
Jamilyn sought his gaze. "You may not
be aware of this, Lachlan, but Fiona
trusted me as a confidante from the
first time we met." She glanced at
Fiona for her approval. "At the church
picnic she confessed her need to find
work and I took it upon myself to make
her quest my own." Her grin turned
smug. "And I have found the perfect
post for you."

"I beg your pardon?" He could
barely remain seated.

"As Lachlan knows—" Jamilyn
flashed him a smile "—I come from a
rather wealthy family. My father may
be a pastor, but his brothers made
their fortunes in Boston, and his
sisters have all married well." He
shifted uncomfortably in his seat.
"And 'twas my family in Boston, if you
remember, Fiona, that I appealed to on
your behalf."

Boston? His eyes fell on Fiona,
but she sat much too engrossed to
notice. What trouble had Fiona
unwittingly set in motion?

"One of my uncles is in desperate
need of a competent horse groomer, and

I assured him you would excel in that post."

"A horse groomer?" He jumped from the sofa.

They both startled.

Let them think his behavior peculiar. He shan't sit still or remain quiet. Fiona wished to breed Quarter Horses, not tend someone else's team.

"Aye, Lachlan. A horse groomer." Jamilyn's eyes narrowed, her expression cross. "She shall work under the stable master, who's a pleasant man," she directed her last comment to Fiona.

"Thank you." Fiona clasped her hands over her knees. "This is more than what I had allowed myself to hope for." His jaw fell open. He looked incredulously between the two women. But, despite him, the conversation proceeded. "When may I start?"

"Post haste."

"I shall depart on Monday then."

"Here, I've written all I know. Directions, names, descriptions, rules, wages, the lot." She delivered her papers to Fiona.

"I truly cannot thank you enough. Me, in Boston," she said incredulously, and glanced up at him. He clamped his jaw shut, and she quickly averted her gaze to his mother, who set the tea service tray down with a clang.

"Did I hear talk of Boston?" his mother clamored.

"Aye." She held up the papers. "I'm to travel there on Monday."

Jamilyn returned to her seat, and boasted, "I secured Fiona a post at one of my uncle's mansions. She shall absolutely adore the home." Her hands moved to exaggerate her words. "The grounds and gardens are simply divine and the house is fit for royalty. The entire estate oozes luxury."

"Jamilyn, she shall be there as a groom." His eyebrows pinched together. "And as such, she shan't be allowed to roam freely. She shall be confined to the stables and paddocks, and even if she were able to roam freely, her days and nights shall be spent working, not strolling or amusing herself."

His mother shot him a look. Aye, his tone may be overly harsh, but

Fiona in Boston? He couldn't fathom it.

"Lachlan." Fiona held his gaze now. "This is a good opportunity for me."

How could she utter such nonsense? Did she not realize how long she would need to work in order to amass enough funds to fulfill her dream of breeding horses—if she could save any money at all?

"I shall be working with horses, instead of taking work as a scullery maid, or some other post where I would toil away my days withindoors." She turned from his glare and smiled at Jamilyn, who accepted a cup of tea from his mother. "I believe I am indebted to you."

"I'm merely satisfied that life shall unfold as intended." Jamilyn waved away her gratitude, then took a sip of her tea and eyed him over the porcelain rim.

A knot twisted in his stomach. Had the pastor's daughter worked with such gusto to distance him from Fiona?

With repugnance, his stomach clenched tighter. "Fiona." He stalked to her chair. "You need not commit to this immediately. Perhaps another—closer—post shall present itself."

"I fear not," Jamilyn decried, with a rattle of her teacup in its saucer. "New Callander is a wee town and I have not heard of a post to match Fiona's equine skills."

His hands fisted.

"Thank you for your concern," Fiona told him. However, he couldn't decipher whether he had annoyed her or she had sought to mollify him. "I cannot remain a guest here indefinitely. I must seek my own source of income."

"Do you possess the funds needed to travel?" Jamilyn cut in. "Because if you require aid, I'm happy to oblige."

"You are most kind to offer assistance. However, I do possess some savings."

Jamilyn's eyebrow rose, and with it, so did his temper. Did she think Fiona penniless? He fumed. Fiona would never be destitute as long as a McAllister lived.

"I propose we leave talk of work and finances." His mother settled herself on the sofa. "I would much rather discuss other matters." She faced Jamilyn. "Have you decided on a gown for tomorrow?"

He knew his mother sought to douse his ire. But she hadn't succeeded. He strode to the oak sideboard and poured himself another cup of tea. His insides simmered hotter than the contents of the teapot.

How could Fiona welcome this opportunity? He marveled at how pleased she seemed to be to leave. Could he do, or say, anything to stop her? Should he even attempt such a thing?

"Lachlan," Fiona murmured beside him. He nearly dropped the teapot. "I apologize for not sharing the details of my conversation with Jamilyn, but I knew not for certain if 'twould amount to anything. She offered to assist me at the picnic and I accepted."

He peered down into anxious flecks of brown and green. She

erroneously thought him angry with
her. "I just—"

"Since you're pouring, Lachlan, I
shall delight in another cup, as
well." Jamilyn smiled, her teacup held
out toward him. He begrudgingly
obliged. "Now, Fiona. Come sit with me
so I may impart my full knowledge of
Boston." She took her arm and leaned
toward her as if in a tête-à-tête,
however her voice boomed, "Lachlan
declared earlier, *when he and I were
alone*, that he has other, more
pressing matters to attend to besides
chattering with us women all
afternoon."

He bit his cheek. But 'twas just
as well that Fiona had been pulled
away. He needed time to calm himself.
"Mama, Fiona, Jamilyn, I thank you for
the tea and company. But, as the only
man present, I fear I may have
overstayed my welcome and seek to
rectify that error." He bowed.

His mother stood. "I must depart,
as well. However, please, do enjoy
yourselves." She smiled down at the
other women. "And thank you for your

visit, Jamilyn. Do give our best to your father."

Jamilyn nodded. "I shall."

He fled the room ahead of his mother and had strode out of the house before he heard her call his name. "Lachlan. I believe 'tis past time we talked."

*L*achlan exhaled with force, as if that action would rid his body of tension. It did not. "What would you like to discuss with me, Mama?" He pinched his nasal bridge and waited for her to converge upon him.

"Fiona."

His eyes slammed shut. He didn't possess the will to discuss her.

"Her acceptance of that post angered you."

He stifled a groan, but ground his teeth. "I simply don't believe she ought to content herself with being a groom in someone else's stable."

"You don't?"

"Nay." He spun and faced his mother. "Not when her dream is to breed horses."

Her hands fisted on her hips. "And can you honestly tell me that is the *only* reason you wish her to refuse that post in Boston?"

"Mama." He harrowed his fingers through his hair. "I understand full well your meaning. You believe I wish her to remain here because I'm in love with her."

"Aye." His mother threw her palms up. "That is precisely what I believe. You've never shown interest in any other lass besides Fiona, and now

she's returned. She's here, Lachlan.
Why would you allow her to leave?"

"*Allow her*?" He let out a heavy
breath. "I don't control her thoughts,
or her actions." His eyes flew to the
house. "Did you not hear her in there?
She wishes to have an income. She's
adamant, despite my objections."

His mother scoffed. "She's
adamant about belonging somewhere.
She's lost her entire family, her
home, her livelihood. She's merely
being sensible. With only herself to
rely on, she must make sure she can
take care of herself. She has had no
other offers presented to her."

"*No other offers*." He shook his
head. "You most certainly are subtle."
He kicked at the dirt and grew silent.

"I fail to understand." His
mother laid her hand on his left arm
and rubbed it gently, obviously
intending not to aggravate his
shoulder wound. She succeeded.
However, his shoulder wound did indeed
aggravate him. "'Tis one thing if you
don't love her, and thus, don't wish
her to be your wife. However, 'tis
another thing entirely, if you do love

her, but something is hindering you from expressing your feelings."

He jerked away from her touch on his inactive arm. "This conversation is pointless. From the moment she arrived, she clearly articulated her desire to leave. And now that an opportunity has presented itself, she's latched on to it." With disgust, he looked at his sling as if 'twere a boa constrictor coiled around him, intent on strangling him. "Her mind is resolved. She's bound for Boston."

His mother crossed her arms. "I believe you've misinterpreted her."

He picked at a loose thread that hung from his sling. "Nay. If she wished to stay, she wouldn't have entreated Jamilyn's help."

"Do you not wonder whether Jamilyn seized upon her request with too much zeal?"

He yanked at the thread and tore it loose. "Again, it matters not. We have only sought to make Fiona feel welcome. We've beseeched her to stay as long as she needs and yet she's chosen to leave at the first opportunity. Surely, you must concede her desire to be rid of us."

"Nay." His mother grabbed his chin. With her fingers pressed into his skin he could look nowhere but at her. "If you love her, tell her. Then, if she leaves, you shall know for certain where her heart lies." Her expression, and her fingers, softened at the emotion she must have seen wither in his eyes. "I believe she would remain, if you supplied her with a reason."

He turned to stare at the distant trees. "I cannot."

"Why ever not?" His mother stood in front of him and blocked his view.

"I have nothing to offer her." He waved his hand around his wounded shoulder. "Look at me."

"Oh, Lachlan—" Concern creased her face, and his body slackened with the knowledge that he had upset her.

"I know my shoulder is healing, but I haven't the faintest notion of how long that shall take. Nor can I ascertain what work I shall do after it heals. I always thought I'd be in the military. Now, I know not what I shall be good for, if anything."

He tried to turn away, but his mother grabbed hold of him. "You listen to me. Some things haven't changed. What's in here certainly has not." She thumped her hand over his heart. "You shall always be the same caring lad, whatever your occupation. And if Fiona loves you, she shall love you under any circumstance."

"Spoken like a good mother."

"Nay. Anyone could validate the truth in my words, even Fiona. Just give her the occasion."

"Mama," he drawled. "She deserves better than a wounded officer, released from duty, with no plans for the future."

"That is for her to determine. Don't settle her mind for her."

"I haven't." He shook his head. "She has accomplished that on her own."

*   *   *

Fiona removed the last rag from her hair and glanced at her newly curled locks in the looking glass. Thoughts of Lachlan kept her seated. She hadn't spoken to him since tea with Jamilyn yesterday, and her stomach twisted at the thought of him still being upset with her.

Although—she clenched hold of another rag—what if he hadn't been angry? Her breath stilled. Could he be saddened by her forthcoming departure?

A thud on her door startled her. "Fiona?" Maisie asked. "Are you dressed for the party?"

"Aye." She calmed herself with a hand down her gown to smooth the fabric as she stood. "Please, enter."

"Oh, Fiona. You are simply radiant."

"Thank you." She curtseyed. "And you are absolutely lovely."

"Thank you." Maisie dipped, as well. "'Tis certainly pleasant to don prettier clothes and rid myself of that apron occasionally."

"I agree." She played with the ribbon above her waist. "I haven't had the opportunity to wear this gown in years."

Maisie crossed the room, and as the distance between them diminished, so did her playfulness. "I realize the men are waiting for us, but before we depart, I must assure you that we in no way wish you to feel as if you must take that appointment in Boston if 'tis not what you truly desire. We do delight in having you here."

"That's kind of you to say." She collected her fan. "However, I believe I have imposed on your hospitality long enough."

"Nonsense. You saved Lachlan's life. You may live here indefinitely, and we still shan't be able to repay you." Maisie looped her arm with hers and they strolled from the room. "Please, consider staying." They descended the stairs. "There may be a good reason for you to remain."

Did that *good reason* include Lachlan? Maisie had voiced her thoughts on the subject before. However, Fiona reminded herself, those were his mother's thoughts, not his.

Her eyes met Lachlan's the moment she stepped out of doors. He stood by the carriage in his finest clothes.

She swallowed—hard—as she admired how his black single-breasted tailcoat flapped over the sides of his dark pantaloons. He wore a cream cravat that matched his waistcoat and socks, which led down to black leather shoes. In a word, he appeared elegant.

"I must say, you are two of the most beautiful women in New Callander." He bowed.

"Thank you for including me in that statement," Maisie joked. "But I believe 'tis Fiona who looks exquisite. Does she not look charming in lavender, Lachlan?"

He nodded and she lowered her gaze to the ground while he helped his mother into the carriage.

"You are, as usual—" he leaned in with a low voice "—stunning."

She forgot to breath. "Thank you," she whispered back. "And you look exceedingly handsome." There. She had been bold, and the smile it produced was definitely worth the effort.

He dipped his chin, then held his right hand out to help her into the carriage. However, when she slipped her fingers into his, she couldn't move.

Could she actually leave for Boston?

Aye.

She stepped up into the carriage. Lachlan's mother had just put fanciful thoughts in her head. She couldn't risk her future on a compliment.

After tonight she would accompany them to church tomorrow, and then say her farewells early Monday morning before she departed—in less than two full days.

She sighed.

*   *   *

"The house is certainly festive." Lachlan admired the vases of fresh flowers, the glowing candelabras, the vast amount of chairs lining the walls, and the rehearsal sounds of the musicians, as he and his grandfather took a turn about the ballroom to scrutinize whether everything was in order before the guests arrived.

"You deserve a grand celebration." His grandfather smiled

as he pushed open the doors that led to the garden. "You and Fiona."

"Fiona most certainly does." He glanced out at the greenery.

His grandfather stilled. "You don't believe you deserve as much?"

He shrugged and pain blasted through his shoulder.

"Joining the military to serve your country rendered us proud." His grandfather walked back into the ballroom with crossed arms and a contemplative face. "But if I recall correctly, you had planned to move up the ranks. Returning home sooner than you expected must be difficult." He nodded from his grandfather's side. "You must realize, however, that even if you had never entered the military, we would still be proud of the man you've become."

"Thank you," he murmured.

"But—" his grandfather urged as he stared at him.

"*But*—" he stroked his sling "—I've grown up hearing stories of Scotland. How your father was a Laird, with a massive kingdom, who fought in the Jacobite Rebellion. Not to mention

274

the heroic feats you yourself accomplished—overcoming torturous years as an indentured servant, risking death for love, and bringing your entire family to the Americas for a better life."

"And you wished to do more?" His grandfather laid a hand on his right shoulder. "You have greatness in you. Still. You always have. Ever since you were a wee lad. You live by God's word, and by His will, you shall accomplish many more wondrous things. Everything I did, I did out of love for your grandmother, and my family, and I see that same drive in you, and Fiona."

With eyebrows pinched together, he mumbled, "You do?"

"Most definitely. Fiona told us how much comfort and help you brought to her homestead, and she risked her life to save you from a battlefield, then left her home to bring you to yours."

A smile crept onto his face. "She is admirable."

"As are you." His grandfather laughed. "Hence, there's no cause for

despair. You have a new life to begin.
You may not be in the military any
longer, but there is much more good
you can do. And at the top of that
would be to wed the love of your life,
the one person God sent especially for
you. Nothing has made me happier or
more content than becoming a husband,
and watching that love grow to make me
a father, and grandfather."

"Perhaps you're correct."

"*Perhaps*?" His grandfather
hitched an eyebrow. "I most definitely
am correct." They laughed as his
grandfather draped his arm around his
back and they strode to the entrance
passageway of the grand three-floor
house.

Fiona stood with his grandmother
and parents, as they waited to greet
guests. With a grin, he took his place
beside her. The question of whether
she was the one God wished him to
marry pounded in his mind. Did she
harbor feelings for him?
He couldn't allow her to leave for
Boston without finding out.

*   *   *

"My, this celebration is fine enough to rival a wedding," the last guest to arrive exclaimed. "Perhaps you ought to marry her tonight, Lachlan?"

His eyes locked on Fiona and she stopped breathing.

"You would save your family additional trouble," the guest continued. "I see the pastor is already in attendance."

With a gracious laugh, Lachlan's grandmother stepped in on their behalf, "When they resolve to marry, we shall be only too happy to host another celebration."

When? Fiona searched Lachlan's face. Why hadn't his grandmother said *if?* Had he told his family something she wasn't privy to?

The sound of bagpipes soared through the air and pivoted her attention. Supper was about to commence. She inhaled the peace and sense of belonging the music transmitted. This way of life was immensely familiar to her. New Callander had been her first home and she had always carried it in her heart.

"As our guests of honor—" his grandmother took her and Lachlan by the hand "—we shall sit you together."

She led them to the most prominent seats and Lachlan pulled out a chair for her. She sat just as Pastor West rose to bless the meal.

"We're gathered here to-day, in honor of these two brave young people." Lachlan raised his hand in thanks as he sat. "As you know, Lachlan fought courageously as an officer in this war. However, what you may not know, is the extent to which he kept his integrity. According to Fiona, he was a beacon of light when her homestead was captured, an honorable man, who worked tirelessly, and not only in his post, but in keeping the soldiers under his command respectable."

She caught Lachlan's eyes on her and smiled. She'd told him numerous times how much she appreciated his presence on her homestead. He shouldn't be shocked that she would tell others of his heroism.

"And Fiona, our long, lost daughter." The pastor turned to her. "Welcome home. You are to be applauded for your courage, as well."

Her eyes grew large and she stared at Lachlan. She had clearly imparted her desire to bury that ugliness with Edgar forever. She didn't wish everyone to know how she had relinquished her homestead, especially the awful reputation she had acquired.

The tightness in her chest diminished with the subtle shake of his head. If he had told Pastor West, he would have also made him promise not to mention the facts she didn't wish to be known publicly.

With her nerves calmed, she smiled at the pastor, and he continued, "Fiona showed tremendous strength bringing Lachlan home alive. And as someone commented to me earlier, if this were a wedding feast, we would all be able to look upon these two with admiration, because the sacrifices they made for each other, are not only humbling, they are rooted in the type of love all marriages should have."

Pastor West dipped his chin at them before he looked toward his daughter's table. "I know I'm delighted to witness such compassion and caring. We must all strive to fight against any selfishness that lies within us and use our energy to help others, as these two have." Jamilyn didn't appear to be listening and he grimaced. "Let us all join hands and bow our heads in prayer."

She joined hands with Cait on her left, and then met Lachlan's amicable eyes. He couldn't extend his injured arm, so she reached across his chest and placed her hand within his.

She felt his warmth under her arm and his fingers grasped hers. He winked at her, then slanted his head in the direction of the other guests. Everyone had already bowed their heads. With a blush of a smile, she tore her eyes from him and pinned her chin to her chest. Thoughts of being his wife swam through her mind as she listened to the pastor pray.

"Amen." Her eyes opened and Cait released her hand. Lachlan, however, held on. Her uncontrollable smile was bashful, but she couldn't pull away.

"Replacing a few details—" Cait's voice shattered their connection, and she withdrew her hand and glanced away from him "—that description of bravery and unselfishness could have described your courtship, Sheena and Logan."

Love still shone in Lachlan's grandparents' gazes. Fiona sighed. Theirs was a *true* love, whereas Pastor West had only speculated about her and Lachlan.

"Aye, there is nothing I shan't have, or still shan't do, for my lassie." Lachlan's grandfather kissed his wife's hand.

"Do you know their story?" Cait asked her.

She shook her head. "Not in its entirety."

"I must tell you over tea sometime."

"Don't omit our courtship that blossomed at the same time." Finnean winked at Cait, then said to Fiona, "Cait was a spirited woman back then."

"*Was*?" Cait shot back. "If you need a reminder that I *still* am, I can most certainly aid you in your education."

They laughed until Lachlan interposed, "Perhaps you should tell Fiona the story now. She's leaving on Monday morning."

"Leaving?" Cait's humorous expression died. "Pray tell, why?"

"I refuse to overstay my welcome."

"Gibberish." Cait waved away her response.

"I need work," she insisted politely. "I've accepted a post in Boston as a horse groomer from one of Jamilyn's uncles."

"*Boston*?" Cait gave Lachlan a sharp look. "That's a considerable distance."

"It most certainly is." He didn't falter under Cait's stare, but Fiona shifted in her seat. "Nevertheless, Fiona is set on it."

"Huh." Cait's grunt echoed with disapproval, but she couldn't say more once Lachlan's grandfather and his brother, Angus, ventured into tales from their childhood in Scotland.

*   *   *

"That was wonderful," Cait declared at the end of the meal. "I especially enjoyed your biscuits, Fiona."

"Thank you." She set down her cutlery. "Each person's contribution definitely made this a fine meal."

"True, and my contribution was to stay away from any, and all, food preparation," Finnean countered, with a grin. "I'm a dreadful disaster in the kitchen."

She laughed, and Lachlan agreed with him, "I can fetch water, tend the fire, and my favorite part is to taste the food, but that's where my skills end. You're fortunate to have married an extraordinary cook. Not only do you have the privilege of eating well, but you know you shall never starve."

Cait's eyes flashed to Fiona. To avoid her, she looked to Lachlan's grandmother, who stood to depart with

the other ladies to the drawing room.
Relieved, she excused herself and
followed Sheena, thankful she had
avoided a discussion that could have
displayed the fond memories she held
of the night she had cooked for
Lachlan and they had sat in front of
her store together.

*   *   *

"Shall we?" Lachlan bowed to
Fiona when she entered the ballroom.
"I would be delighted." She put
her white gloved hand in his and he
led her to the dancers that had
assembled. Soon Sir Watkins' Jig had
everyone twirling, jumping, and
spinning in circles. She laughed as
they weaved between the other couples.
"Your foot work is more than adept,
Lachlan."

He dipped his chin with a playful
grin, and pulled her away from a near
collision with a dancer in the next
group. "My cousin, Blair, never did
take to dancing."

She grinned and twirled away.
When she came back to him, he took her

hand and gave it a gentle squeeze. Her eyes locked with his. If only this song would last all night.

"Lachlan." Jamilyn flounced beside them when the music stopped. His head was still lowered in his bow. "I do believe you promised me a dance."

Fiona lost her equilibrium as she rose from her curtsey. But she straightened her thoughts, and her lavender gown, quickly. "Please, enjoy yourselves. Lachlan is a most impressive dancer." She spun on her heel and walked to the outskirts of the room.

"Would you honor me with a dance?" Blair asked before she could seat herself.

"I'd be the one honored." She took his hand and he led her into the line before the next song, Dressed Ship, began to play. 'Twas a lively tune. And she laughed along with Blair at his fumbled steps.

But as the couples twirled and jumped, they rotated partners, until she was again across from Lachlan and their hands were joined. "You light up the ballroom," he said, before he danced off in another direction.

She smiled at the partner that presented himself, but her eyes turned sharply to Lachlan's. She took a deep breath, forced to twirl farther away from him once more, until finally she reached Blair for the song's conclusion.

"Are you in need of some refreshment?" he asked.

She nodded. It hadn't escaped her notice that Jamilyn had clutched hold of Lachlan and fully intended to stand up with him again.

The musicians played, Prince George's Birthday song. "Lachlan told me how tremendously pleased you were to view the house my parents' bequeathed me." Blair handed her a glass.

She thanked him. "Aye, thank you. That's where I was born, and raised until I was fifteen." She sipped her drink. "You don't intend to make it your home?"

"Nay, I'm comfortably settled on another property I own." He lifted his drink at a friend who danced past them.

"Lachlan said the homestead was for sale. Please do not think me bold, but I am curious, how much do you hope to sell it for?"

"Actually." He smirked. "I've just sold it."

"Oh." The air gushed from her lungs.

"Aye, the purchaser was most ardent." A coy smile slid across his face.

She dipped her chin. "I'm glad you found someone who shall cherish the property as it deserves. I'm happy the matter was settled so amicably for you both."

"Thank you." He grinned.

"I hope I'm not intruding?" Lachlan glanced between them.

"Nay, of course not." Blair bowed to her and thanked her for her company. "I do hope you shall reconsider remaining in New Callander. 'Twould indeed please some of us immensely." The right side of his lip curled and she looked between the men.

Blair winked at Lachlan and her stomach flipped.

"Will you take a turn about the garden with me?" Lachlan asked.

"Aye." She set down her glass on a tray, before he offered his good arm and they strolled out of doors, away from the party.

14

"I do wish you would reconsider not taking work in Boston," Lachlan's voice was even, as they walked along the garden path.

Fiona stole a glance at him. He
didn't meet her eyes. "I don't see how
I could possibly refuse the work," she
rambled. "I may not receive another
offer this agreeable, and I need to
begin work again. I must save money to
eventually breed Quarter Horses. That
is still my dream."

"Is it?" In earnest, he finally
beheld her. "I believed life in the
military was my dream, but now I'm not
certain that's why I pursued being an
officer. Perhaps I used the military
to fulfill a part of me I couldn't
complete in any other way." His pace
slowed and his eyes rested on their
entwined arms. "Earlier, I spoke with
my grandfather. He reminded me of what
is truly important in life. And 'tis
something I never thought I could have
before. However, now—" his eyes
traveled up to meet hers "—I may be
able to."

She looked away from his intense
gaze, into the darkness on the
horizon. "I'm glad for you. And
although I cannot deny that I wish
things were different and I could
stay—"

"That's precisely my point. Is your dream to breed horses or has your dream been to return here, to the life you used to know?"

With a stop, she pulled her arm from his. Her mind whirled. "I've never entertained such thoughts. When I lived here, my family still lived and 'twas the happiest time of my life. Could I have tied that longing into my dream of breeding Quarter Horses? Nearly all my leisure time was spent at Finnean and Cait's."

She plucked at her long white gloves and stretched them farther above her elbows. "You've definitely given me much to consider." How could she ever have agreed to leave here again? "Being here has felt akin to returning home. 'Tis as if an empty hole inside my heart is refilling."

He stepped toward her. Her hands and her breathing stilled. She looked up at him. "Then stay." He stood mere inches from her now. She could no longer feel the breeze between them.

"But I've already promised Jamilyn."

"Jamilyn and her uncle shall understand."

"I don't know." She shook her head and fidgeted with her gloves again. "This is all so sudden. I haven't had time to think through any of this."

"Fiona." He gently rose her chin until her eyes met his. "I shan't push you into a decision. But please, promise to pray about this tonight." His brown eyes roamed her face. "Say you shall speak to me about it again tomorrow."

"I shall," she murmured.

"Good." He smiled. Then after a lingering moment he pulled his hand away. "Will you permit me to show you something I think you shall enjoy?"

She tilted her head. Her eyes squinted. "You have become a man with many hidden surprises."

"I always was." A light danced in his eyes. "*You* were simply too young to notice."

She laughed and swatted at him with her fan. "Mind your manners, young man." He pulled back with a grin and avoided her teasing wrath.

Why had she ever considered their difference in age detrimental? She shook her head at her younger self. A year or two, or even several more, mattered not. Lachlan was simply Lachlan. Her dearest friend.

However, when he took her hand and they began to walk once more, her heart thumped against her chest, and she knew he meant more to her than a friend.

"Here we are." He led her to a row of green bushes covered with tightly closed buds.

"And why have we stopped here?"

"'Tis almost dusk." His lip jerked upward.

"I can see that. 'Tis all the more reason to return to the ballroom. I shan't wish for rumors to begin circulating about us. And besides, the mosquitoes shall soon delight in feeding upon us."

"Please." He squeezed her hand. "Humor me for a few moments more."

She raised a brow, then smiled. "Fine. But, you are most definitely a genuine man of mystery."

"Just watch the bushes." He chuckled, and looked down the length of them.

"I fail to see anything," she began to protest.

"Just watch." He shook his head. "There." He pointed to a yellow flower she hadn't seen blooming on the bush only seconds before. "This is the one flower I actually know the name of—Evening Primrose."

She stared at the bushes and the flowers came alive.

"Every time I stand here watching them erupt into a wall of flowers, I feel as if God has put on a show just for me."

"I've never seen anything so beautiful." Within ten minutes, all the buds had popped open and the darkness of night became illuminated by darling little yellow flowers.

"I knew you would appreciate it." He stepped in closer and shivers ran through her as his hand traveled across her upper back and rested on her shoulder.

She looked up at him and their eyes locked. Her body turned into him

and his hand warmed the back of her
neck.

"Fiona." He brushed her cheek.
His fingers settled in her hair. She
couldn't breathe as his lips came ever
so slowly down.

He was going to kiss her.

Her knees weakened.

She wished for nothing more than
to kiss him. Even if 'twould be their
one and only kiss. A farewell kiss to
cherish for the rest of her life.

"Lachlan." His name echoed
through the night, but it hadn't come
from her lips. "Lachlan."

She pulled away. His gaze still
held hers—with force. "Fiona," he
whispered. "I don't wish you to go."

She searched his face. Did he
mean at this exact moment or ever?

"I must." She hastened back
toward the lights of the ballroom. She
knew from her experience in Queenston
what it meant to be the object of
gossip and she didn't wish for that
ugliness here.

"There you are, Lachlan,"
Jamilyn's voice filled the garden, as
she crept farther away.

Lachlan peered into the darkness, but Fiona was gone. He yearned for more time with her. However, that was a luxury he didn't possess. She would only be here one more day. And tomorrow was Sunday. They must attend church. He grimaced and rubbed the back of his neck. Tomorrow was also Independence Day. They would be alone even less than he wished.

"Lachlan, why are you in the garden?" Jamilyn clucked her tongue. "Surely, the guest of honor ought to be in attendance at his own party." He faced her. His expression must have been grave, because her smile faded. "You appear to be in the depths of some considerably serious thought."

He nodded. He was overwhelmed. A week and a half ago his life was simple—strive to be the best officer, move up the ranks, and make his family proud. But then he found Fiona, became injured, nearly died, was discharged from the military, and came home with the woman he once thought he'd marry.

Could all that have been God's plan? Did He bring them together, not just so that Lachlan could protect Fiona, or that she could save his life, but to give them a second chance at love?

"Would you care to tell me what you're thinking? If I can, I do indeed desire to help." She put her hand on his forearm.

With an intentionally sharp turn, that caused her hand to fall from his arm, he set his gaze upon the evening primrose. "I was pondering the future."

"I adore dreaming about the future." She picked a yellow blossom. "Being married to the most handsome man, having the loveliest home, spending my days blissfully happy." She sighed and smelled the flower as she looked up at him.

"You didn't mention children. Are they not part of your dreams?" He could imagine Fiona as a mother. The mother of *his* children. She'd faithfully tend them, nourish them, and make certain they felt loved.

"*Children*? Of course. I assumed they were implied." She laughed. "But enough about my dreams. Now that you're no longer in the military, what are your plans for the future?"

He hesitated. He hadn't revealed them to anyone. Nevertheless, he could think of no reason not to share his news. He had definitely set his mind on this goal, and he would tell Fiona as soon as he could. "I've decided upon breeding horses."

The yellow petals fell from her fingers. "Is that not what Fiona declared her dream to be?"

"Aye." He smiled.

For a moment she considered him in silence. "Oh, I understand. How astute you are. Once Fiona is settled in Boston she shan't be your competition." She plucked another flower. "I'm certain you shall be successful, however, if you need any help, I shall be more than happy to assist you."

"You've misunderstood me." He straightened his cravat. He didn't wish to hurt Jamilyn, and yet he couldn't let her believe that he didn't love Fiona. 'Twould be best if she knew. Perhaps then she could set her affections toward someone else.

Hopefully, Cole. "I mean to breed horses *with* Fiona."

Her mouth fell open. "But she's to live in Boston and be a horse groomer. My uncle is expecting her."

"My most ardent hope is that she shall reconsider. Because I wish my future to coincide with hers. Having her in my life, by my side, has always been my dream."

Her eyebrows pinched together and she stared at him for several moments before she spoke again, "Am I to understand that you haven't asked her to stay yet?"

He rubbed his chin. "Nay, not yet. I plan to ask her tomorrow following church."

"Oh." She slowly nodded. "But what if she refuses? 'Twould pain me to see you hurt. You've only been acquainted with this lass for less than a fortnight."

"That's not entirely accurate. I've known her my whole life. We may have been separated, but I believe she's remained the same."

"You cannot be certain of that. And you were a mere lad when she lived here previously. You didn't actually witness her maturation. Unlike how we grew together."

"That may be true. However, my heart doesn't understand such disparity. I'm compelled to declare my feelings to her. I cannot allow her to leave otherwise."

"But if she loved you, would she not have immediately refused that post in Boston?"

"Perhaps. But again, I'm led by my heart, and it wishes a full confession. I once believed that God placed Fiona on this earth to be my wife, and whenever I thought of myself married, with a family, she was the lass in those dreams."

"Fine, but if she refuses you, will you finally let your childish dreams die and take a wife who does love you?"

His gaze plunged to the black dirt. Her rejection would hurt worse than the pain he had suffered near death. Nevertheless. "Fiona has, and shall always, remain my one and only true love. Whether or not she loves me in return, does not alter that."

"Absurd. If she hasn't the sense to love you, then you ought to bid her farewell and find someone who does."

"Once more, you may be correct. However, that's not how my feelings are fashioned. I love Fiona Robertson." He smiled, despite how her face creased with distaste. To have spoken those words, invigorated him. Ever louder, he wished to yell his declaration.

But for now, he needed to content himself with organizing some arrangements.

"*L*achlan, do you know where I might find Jamilyn?" Cole, Cait and Finnean's grandson, met him in his grandparent's vestibule the moment he returned to the celebration.

"She's in the garden." His lips twitched up at the grin that spread over his friend's face. If Cole felt even a fraction of how he felt toward Fiona, he understood the man's eagerness to locate her.

"Thank you." His friend tapped him on the back as their mutual cousin, Blair sauntered in.

"Where is Cole bounding off to?"

"Chasing love," he chuckled. "Just as I am. Hence why, I must thank you again for selling me your parents' homestead."

"'Tis my sincerest wish that you shall enjoy a blessed life there." He winked at him. "Fiona inquired about it earlier and I told her I had sold it."

His heart skipped. "You didn't reveal that you had sold it to me?"

"Nay." His cousin shook his head with a laugh. "Your secret is safe with me."

"Good." His heart returned to its normal rhythm. "For I wish to surprise her with that house."

"Have you concocted a plan?"

"Aye," he beamed. "I adore Fiona. And tomorrow, I shall not only tell her that, I shall ask her to be my wife.

"Congratulations!" A clap fell on his good shoulder.

"Blair, please, lower your voice." His eyes darted about in every direction. No one appeared to have heard their conversation. "'Tis to be a surprise, remember."

"Of course. I apologize." He covered his smile with both hands. "But don't fear. That's another secret that shall remain safe with me."

"Thank you. However, I did hope you might do more than merely keep my secrets?"

"Oh?" He smirked with a raised a brow. "What do you need from me?"

"My plan is to propose to Fiona in her family's former home. However, for my plan to succeed, someone must bring her to the house after church, where I shall wait in surprise."

"'Twould be my honor to help." They shook hands, and he thanked him before his cousin rejoined the party.

"Lachlan, why are you not dancing?" His grandmother took hold of his arm. "Is anything the matter?"

He looked between her and her best friend, Cait, and shook his head as a smile spread over his lips. "On the contrary. I believe I'm on the cusp of something wonderful."

"Do tell us about that." Cait fanned herself.

"Aye, let us share in your happiness," his grandmother agreed.

"Only if you both promise to keep my secret?" He eyed them with false scrutiny.

They laughed. "What a question to ask *us*?" Cait closed her fan.

"I'm in love with Fiona."

Both women squealed with delight. "Have you told her?" his grandmother asked. He shook his head.

"Why ever not?" Cait shook her fan at him. "Go to her this minute."

"Nay," he chuckled. "I shall tell her, tomorrow—when I propose."

Both women sighed with delight. "Oh, Lachlan. I cannot express my joy." His grandmother hugged him. "I wish you both an abundance of God's blessings."

"As do I." Cait hugged him next.

"Thank you, but she hasn't given her consent."

"Oh, she shall." His grandmother patted his arm. "In her eyes I see how immensely bright her love for you shines." He prayed his grandmother was correct.

"I've seen it as well." Cait nodded. "Ergo, you must plan for when she agrees to become your beautiful bride."

"I have." He grinned. "I've already purchased her family's former homestead. And since her deepest desire is to breed Quarter Horses, I secured a mare."

"Thoughtful, compassionate, and considerate, she shan't refuse you." His grandmother hugged him again.

"Correct me if I'm wrong," Cait interposed. "But do you not also require a stallion?"

"Aye." He took a deep breath. "However, after purchasing the homestead and mare, I have insufficient funds for a proper stallion."

His grandmother patted his hand. "Not to worry. Your grandfather and I shall supply one as a wedding present."

"We couldn't accept such a lavish gift."

"Aye, you can, and you shall." His grandmother shook her head and laughed. "Because nothing would please us more than to witness you happily married."

"And if you require any assistance," Cait added. "Finnean and I shall only be too glad to aid you. Consider our stables at your disposal."

With his mouth agape, he looked from one to the other. "I shall never be able to adequately thank you."

"Oh, pish." Cait waved.

"'Tis our pleasure." His grandmother kissed his cheek. "And don't even dare think of repaying us. Someday, soon, you shall beget your own children, and grandchildren, and you can do unto them."

Cait nodded in agreement.

"I shall still thank you both every day for the rest of my life."

"Fine," Cait laughed. "But do bring us your babies to hug, kiss, and spoil when you do."

Fiona sipped her drink as she watched the dancers twirl about the ballroom. The evening had been extraordinary. And the more she thought about what Lachlan had said to her in the garden, the more she realized he was correct.

She may have loved horses, and her time at Cait and Finnean's farm when she was younger, but she had never wished to breed horses then. She had only ever dreamed of having her own family with a man she cherished. 'Twasn't until she was sent away that she developed her ambitious Quarter Horse breeding goal. And now she was certain that dream emerged to provide her with a similar life to the one she had left behind—and dearly missed. Somehow Lachlan had deciphered that. Somehow he knew her better than she knew herself.

Stepping back into New Callander, she had returned to the home she had only been able to gain admittance to in her dreams. Why had she ever agreed to leave? She must tell Jamilyn she couldn't go to Boston.

"Jamilyn." She glided across the ballroom to her. "I must speak with you regarding my work in Boston."

Jamilyn's lips formed a taut line. "Aye, we do indeed need to discuss your departure."

"Allow me to begin—"

"Actually, I must insist upon being heard first." The pastor's daughter tucked her arm into hers.

"Fine." Her eyebrows pinched together. "Please, proceed."

Jamilyn lowered her head toward her and spoke in a hushed tone, "Do you recall my telling you about a friend I write to in Queenston?"

She nodded. "Miss Penelope Sherwood."

"Aye." Jamilyn eyed some nearby guests, then pulled her farther into seclusion. "In response to mine, I received a letter from my friend. She was thoroughly forthright in her revelation of information about you."

"Why might that have caused your tone to become sinister?"

"Because Penelope informed me about you."

She simply stared at her.

"Please don't force me to utter such vile words, Fiona."

"I apologize, but I cannot falsely claim to understand what you're alluding to."

"Your reputation," the pastor's daughter sneered. "Penelope revealed how you're known in Queenston as a woman of, oh how can I say this delicately, immorality."

"*Immorality*?" she screeched. "Jamilyn, I assure you, I am not immoral."

"Everyone in Queenston is aware that men remained at your homestead overnight while you were unchaperoned."

Her hand flew to her hip, she now understood her full well. "My homestead was captured by American soldiers. And as God as my witness, I did not act with any indecency."

"Please compose yourself. I shall not argue the facts with you. My sole intent was to warn you of their consequences." She grabbed her arm again and dragged her into the shadows of a tall plant.

"The *consequences*?" she hissed. "What consequences?"

"The ridicule that shall befall Lachlan." Jamilyn released her arm. "Your time alone with him in the garden this evening did not go unnoticed." Her new friend grimaced, as if a foul odor had blown into their secluded corner of the room. "Rumors have already begun to circulate about your relations since you dwell under the same roof. And now you've been seen in the dark of night, alone together."

"Lachlan and I are not cohabitating. I'm a guest in his *parents'* home. I have my own room. And nothing untoward happened in the garden tonight."

"There's no need to justify yourself to me. But you must understand that your reputation hurts Lachlan."

She stood speechless. She could never knowingly hurt him.

"You must acknowledge that you are ruining his good name. His association with you bestows shame upon him."

Her eyes moistened.

"If you care for him, you shall stay away from him and leave immediately."

The air grew heavy and she blinked rapidly. Her unshed tears blurred her vision. She felt everyone's glare upon her.

"All is not destroyed though. I shall help you." Jamilyn laid a hand on her shoulder. "I shall arrange for a coach to transport you to Boston tomorrow. Sit with me during church service, and before it finishes, we shall slip out unnoticed." When she hesitated, Jamilyn leaned in closer. "This ought not to pose a problem for you, since you had planned on departing Monday morning anyway. This simply reduces the length of time which Lachlan shall be exposed to the horrendous rumors and ugliness that surround you."

She gaped at her. She had decided against going.

"'Tis the only way to ensure that people forget you. Then Lachlan can proceed with his life unharmed, as if you never existed." Her words struck with the power of a bayonet through the heart. "Do you understand the direness of this matter?"

She floundered a nod.

"Good. Then, shall you allow Lachlan to live the life he was meant to, or shall you impede him?"

She bit her lip. If her departure absolved him, she would most willingly go. She couldn't subject him to such scorn. If she was tainted by scandal, she could never allow that to stain him. She would do anything for him.

"I shall sit beside you in church tomorrow," she blurted. She couldn't bear to hear anyone gossip about her or Lachlan. She wouldn't be confronted with the same ridicule she had received on the street in Queenston when she had gone to purchase that mutton.

"I'm glad." Jamilyn looked toward the dancers. "This shall be best for everyone."

She opened her mouth, but her protest died into a gurgle. Jamilyn was correct. Everywhere she looked, people stared at her. She knew their vile thoughts, and ran from the ballroom.
Jamilyn's words reverberated in her head as she fled the house.

People had declared those exact words throughout her entire life. Being sent to live in Upper Canada, would *be best for everyone*. Marrying Doctor Edgar Blackstone, would *be best for everyone*. And now this! How come what was purported to be *best for everyone*, never appealed to her?

She dashed to the stables. Underneath a cloak of humidity, the air had cooled. However, she was determined to locate the McAllister's horses and wait with those civilized beasts until the evening's festivities ended.

She lifted her skirts. The hay and dirt soiled her shoes, but she paid them no mind. With a heavy heart, she dragged her feet past each stall.

"I knew I'd find you here."

She dropped her skirts. "Lachlan, why are you not dancing?"

A smile played on his face. "Because you're not there to dance with me." He leaned on the gate of his horse's stall.

Face averted, she stroked the bay's spotted muzzle, as the animal bumped into her shoulder.

"Horses do love you." He gave the brown beauty a pat.

"The feeling is mutual." She let her hand drop and stepped back.

He launched himself out of the stall. "Was I mistaken, then?"

"To what do you refer?" She walked to the stable's opening, her eyes on the hay she crushed underfoot.

"Our discussion regarding the reason you wished to breed horses."

She stopped at the stable door. She didn't wish to discuss this, but she had promised, and would keep her word. "I've missed living here." Not able to meet his honest eyes, she glanced up as far as his cravat.

"Especially my family. More so than I could ever allow myself to be sensible of."

"And now that you recognize this, has your dream been affected?"

Her eyes locked on his. She still adored horses. However, her dream had changed. He was now the center of her dreams. And yet, the reputation she had been slandered with prevented her from expressing her true feelings.

"I must confess that my dream of breeding horses may have been nothing more than a way to placate myself. You helped me understand that, and I thank you. Now I must accept the reality that is my life. I'm to be a horse groomer in Boston." She tightly clasped her hands. "That's the life God has provided for me. And I shall appreciate it."

"Fiona." He took hold of her elbow. "You may seek a different course for your life. You need not go to Boston unless you wish to." His face communicated more concern than she could bear. Her stomach clenched. But she must bid him farewell.

Is this how he felt that night at her homestead before he left for battle? She yearned to embrace him. To feel him hold her and make her feel safe, as if the world didn't exist and only the two of them remained.

But that could never be. She shan't allow him to be cast aside for his dealings with a woman believed to be unchaste. "I appreciate all you've done for me. And whenever I think of you, it shall always be with the most affectionate memories. But, I must go to Boston."

"Allow me to dissuade you."

She placed two fingers upon his warm lips and shook her head. "Please. Not tonight." His enlivened eyes fought with hers. However, no time remained for his campaign. Footsteps thumped above the croak of frogs.

She yanked her fingers away and stepped back. She couldn't be caught alone with him—again. "I'm sorry." She scampered out into the darkness of the night.

achlan's eyes flew open. 'Twas the fourth of July. The day he would ask the woman he had always loved to marry him. His heart raced, and he jumped from his bed to keep pace with it.

Before the rest of the household awoke, he crept out of the house to walk to the one he had purchased for Fiona. Hope blossomed in his heart as the sun began to shine and the temperature rose. 'Twas as if nature smiled with him.

After he picked the same flowers he had helped her gather on the day of the picnic, he placed them in jars, and spread them throughout the house with a numbered note beside each one.

He could foresee her walk from bouquet to bouquet as she read his amorous notes. Then, the last note would usher her out the backdoor where he would secretly await her on bended knee. Just the thought of that moment required him to inhale a sharp breath.

He kissed the last note, then propped it on the table. Only a few hours remained until she graced him with an answer. How would he sit still through church with the knowledge of what was to happen after?

Fiona awoke with a groan. Thoughts of her attempt to say goodbye to Lachlan last night had scraped her raw. She rolled over and hugged her mother's quilt. To-day she would, once again, begin her life anew. And she dreaded every moment.

With a firm voice however, she commanded herself to sit at her table. The need to write him a letter impelled her. Last night's words simply couldn't be her last ones to him.

She scribbled furiously. Then with a sigh, she folded the paper and placed it on her bed. *God, please help him understand why I must proceed in such a manner.* She grabbed her valise, and while the McAllister's slept, she slipped down the stairs.

With two biscuits tucked away, she skulked out of the kitchen. Tears fell before she even reached the carriage and threw in her traveling receptacle.

In vain, she swatted at the droplets while she concealed her belongings under the carriage's blankets, but her sadness gushed forth. She must leave Lachlan, the McAllisters, her birthplace, and the last remaining member of her family—her dog, Scolty.

He would enjoy a better life here. But every step she took toward the barn made her heart squeeze tighter in her chest. "Scolty," her voice broke as she entered the barn. He bounded to her with his tail wagging, and she nearly smothered him. "Be a good dog for Lachlan." She kissed his snout. "Watch over him for me."

The dog tilted his head as if he understood. With a sob, she scratched the softness behind his ears. "You're a hero." She embraced him and he licked her face. "I shall miss you dearly," she cried into his sable fur. "But you shall live in my heart forever."

She couldn't rub away her tears, and fumbled through her blurred vision to offer Scolty the last biscuit she would ever feed him. "Good dog." She stroked his head. Scolty prized her with a panting smile before he trotted away to follow Lachlan's farm dog out of the barn.

She stood on trembling legs. She needed strength, and turned to God in prayer before she shook the dirt from the bottom of her gown and traipsed out of the barn.

Her path back to the house was lined with Queen Anne's Lace. She sighed as she picked one and stroked its delicate white surface. This flower would always remind her of Lachlan, and home.

She spun on her heel. The urge to behold her family's old homestead one final time choked her tears.

Lachlan peered up from the path he followed toward his parents' home. His steps faltered. A woman's form stood ahead of him. "Fiona," he called, with a wave. He would recognize her anywhere. The way she moved, with her light brown hair falling over her shoulders, as her gown swayed with the contours of her body while she walked—beautiful.

"Lachlan?" She froze. "I didn't expect to encounter anyone along this trail." She studied him. "Were you visiting my former home?"

He nodded, but walked past her, then thanked God when she followed him. He couldn't allow her to stumble upon his preparations. They had church to attend first. "You're a vision of loveliness this morning."

"Thank you." She didn't meet his eyes.

Did she not welcome his compliments? He shoved his hands in his pockets. "Are my parents set to depart? It must be nearing that time."

"I wouldn't know." Her gaze remained over her shoulder at her family's old homestead.

"If you wish to visit it once more, I can arrange for my cousin to accompany you after church?" He held his breath. Her agreement was imperative to the success of his plan.

"Blair?" Her head swung forward.

"Aye, until the new owner takes residence he is still in possession of the key."

She shook her head. "No need to trouble him."

"I'm certain he'd be glad to accompany you. Trust me. You may go with him directly after church." He hoped she didn't notice how his voice had quickened with an eagerness he couldn't squash.

"There you both are," his mother's exasperated tone burst over the land as heavy as her footfalls. "We were debating whether we ought to wait or leave without you."

Perhaps he ought to have written his mother a note as to his whereabouts. "Sorry, Mama." He smiled to himself. If his mother only knew how many notes he had written that morning.

"Aye, I apologize, as well." Fiona stood as a contradiction to him. Her face soured with worry and concern.

"No need." His mother spun on her heel and called over her shoulder, "We need to depart now though, for if we don't, I fear we shall arrive markedly late."

He eyed Fiona. "Are you prepared to leave?" She took a deep breath and finally nodded.

He kept his pace slow, and the distance between them and his mother grew considerably. "Fiona, are you troubled by something?" She shook her head, but failed to convince him. Her countenance betrayed her, but they reached the carriage with him none the wiser.

He helped her up, then sat beside her. She glanced behind, face forlorn, as the carriage rolled to church. "Thank you for allowing me respite in your home," she propelled her words to the front of the carriage where his parents sat. "You've been most generous and kind."

"No need to thank us, my dear," his mother replied.

Fiona remained rigid. She sat upright with her face taut, as if this journey would end with her execution.

He leaned closer to her. "You do realize 'tis I who ought to thank you every moment of everyday for saving my life."

She stared at him, her hazel eyes large. "Lachlan," she uttered his name as if it burned her tongue. "I believe you erroneously inverted our situations. Had it not been for you, I am without a doubt that Edgar would have ascertained some other torturous scheme to force me from his uncle's land, and then I would have been alone in my dealings with him."

He rested his hand on hers. "My gratitude to God shall never cease for allowing my regiment to capture your homestead and thus bring us together."

The faintest smile touched her lips. "I shall always be thankful, as well, and I shan't fail to cherish the memory of this time."

He squeezed her hand and reminded himself that she spoke in this manner because she still planned to depart tomorrow morning. He fought within himself, his heart wished to propose then and there, his head however, demanded he follow his plan.

"We've arrived," his mother beamed. "And I do believe we shan't be considered tardy."

Fiona pulled her hand away from his and brushed a stray strand of hair from her cheek. She no longer appeared even the slightest bit calm. Her features froze with dread and her demeanour was grim.

Perhaps she aggrieved the thought of her departure tomorrow. He assisted her down from the carriage. If that were true, his heart leapt at the thought of her reaction to his proposal.

"Fiona." Jamilyn flounced forward and took her by the arm. "I hope you shall sit with me to-day?"

Fiona nodded.

He didn't protest. As much as he wished to remain near her, this afforded him the opportunity to solidify his plan with Blair.

He bowed to her. "We shall speak later." He subdued his tone to mask a heart which threatened to explode with the surprise he harbored.

She didn't acknowledge him. Jamilyn pulled her away too soon.

"Don't cry," Jamilyn's voice failed to soothe her, even as she rubbed her arm.

The unshed tears burned. She wouldn't cry. She had already shed enough tears. And, she reminded herself firmly, she must do this for Lachlan. To save his reputation. To ensure he could live a good life here.

"Are you prepared for your departure?" the pastor's daughter whispered, after they had sat in the back pew.

She nodded. "My valise is hidden in the McAllister's carriage."

"Excellent, we shall move it to my carriage before I drive you to catch the coach destined for Boston." Her friend straightened to shield her from sight as someone passed by.

She knew she appeared distraught, but that was irrevocable. She only had mere minutes left in New Callander. Her eyes sought Lachlan. Handsome, courageous, strong, and caring, he stood in a discussion with his cousin, Blair.

God, I don't profess to comprehend Your reason for allowing any of this to occur. And 'twould be a lie if I didn't proclaim a desire for things to be different. She folded her hands on her lap in prayer. However, she didn't close her eyes. *God, please understand my need to see Lachlan during these final moments. These memories shall be all I have to remember him in the lonely days, and years, ahead. Oh, how I wish I could remain here. Marry Lachlan. Have a family again.*

Her concentration was wrenched away by people who stared and whispered. She held in her frustration. Now more than ever, she recognized the need for her actions. He didn't deserve to be sullied by her atrocious reputation.

The service began, and despite the gossip, she stole several more glances at him, for by sundown, she wouldn't even be in the Mohawk Valley.

"'Tis time," Jamilyn murmured.

She swallowed and took a deep breath. Her stomach roiled and her heart splintered. *Goodbye, my love.* She tore her eyes from him and slunk out of the church behind Jamilyn.

When the service finished, Lachlan turned in his seat to search for Fiona. He didn't see her. She must have already exited the church. She had been sitting closest to the door.

"Lachlan." Blair stood at his side. "At your command, I shall commence with the plan."

"Then I shall leave directly. However, if you encounter any difficulty bringing Fiona to the house, entreat my grandmother or your great-aunt for help. They've been apprised of my plan and Fiona shan't refuse them." He grinned. "Although, with the amount of winks and smiles I've received, not to mention all the whispering, I believe the entire community knows my intent of asking her to marry me to-day. They've been staring at us throughout this entire service." He rubbed his chin. "I do hope their banter didn't reach Fiona's ears?"

"Don't fret. Steer your mind toward your goal, and what needs doing, and forget everyone and everything else." He clapped him on the back. "I shall deliver her to you. Now go."

*   *   *

Lachlan wiped his forehead. He couldn't remain still. He paced the entire length of the back of the house more times than he could count as he rehearsed his words. Then he froze. The sound of horses' hooves approached.

God, please help me express my love to Fiona properly so she knows how deeply I love her and shall always cherish her.

His heart stopped as footsteps neared the front of the house. The door opened and closed.

He attempted to calculate the length of time she would need to read the notes before she reached him.

He lowered himself to one knee.

The backdoor opened.

His breath caught in his lungs.

Please, God, let her consent to becoming my wife.

"Blair?" Lachlan's jaw went slack. "Where's Fiona?" He stood and looked past his cousin. "Could you not convince her to come?"

"I was not provided with an opportunity to even try." He pursed his lips. "I couldn't ascertain her whereabouts."

His knees weakened. "Did you search the graveyard?"

Blair nodded.

"The waterfall?"

Another nod. "I searched everywhere. I made inquiries with everyone. No one saw her after the service."

He resumed his pacing. "Where could she have gone?"

"I know not. But there's something else you ought to know."

He stopped and whipped himself around at his cousin's ominous tone. "Please, reveal what you know," he pleaded when Blair stalled.

"Jamilyn was nowhere to be seen either."

Jamilyn? He raked his fingers through his hair. She had insisted that Fiona sit with her. However, he doubted Fiona would spend her final hours with her instead of with him or his family. "Do you actually believe she's with Jamilyn?"

His cousin shrugged.

His face fell into his hand and he rubbed the tension. He glanced at the sky before his eyes rested on Blair. "Will you help me find her?"

"You need not ask. Shall I search for them at Jamilyn's home?"

"Aye, and I shall drive through town, then back past the church. Perhaps they went into the woods." They strode to their carriages. "If you find her, please bring her to my parents' house, and if not, we shall meet there at suppertime to devise a new plan." Blair tipped his hat, and Lachlan climbed into his carriage.

He knew not why such an urgent need to find her surged through him. She couldn't be in danger—at least he prayed she wasn't. And yet, revolting thoughts of what might have happened to her gnawed at him.

He set off. His heart pounded in his ears. Ahead of him, Blair slowed his horses. "Lachlan," his parents shouted as they ran toward him with their arms waving.

He jumped down, and shuddered at
the pain that shot through his
shoulder.

"Here." His mother pushed papers
into his stomach. His father hunched
over, hands on his thighs. Both were
completely out of breath. "They're
from Fiona." His mother grabbed her
side, which appeared to be pinching
her. "We received a letter, as well. A
thank you note for allowing her to
reside with us."

"Prepare yourself, son" his
father huffed. "I believe she's
gone—for good."

His eyes darted between his
parents before he tore the letter
open. What was happening?

Dearest Lachlan,
I apologize for not bidding you
goodbye in person. Please don't
think unkindly of me. Forgive my
actions. My departure was
intended to be beneficial, not
harmful. I left church early,
because fortunately, Jamilyn
arranged for me to travel on a
coach directly to Boston.

As you may have guessed, I have not brought Scolty with me. As much as I wished to, I know he shall be happier with you on the farm. However, if you cannot care for him, I will understand. Jamilyn can provide you with the details of my whereabouts. Simply write to me and I shall send for him.

But I caution you, refrain from seeking any other communication with me. Jamilyn has informed me that my reputation from Queenston has followed me to New Callander, and I do not wish you tainted by it.

I can only hope that I shall be unhampered by it in Boston. However, the more I think on it, the more I am convinced of its impossibility. I shall be working in Jamilyn's uncle's house, and if Jamilyn was able to gain that knowledge, word may spread there, as well.

Hence, I shall seek work elsewhere as soon as I am able. Somewhere farther away, where no one knows me. Perhaps out west. Then I can finally be free.

And that, Lachlan, is what I wish for you—a happy life. I

shall pray that God blesses you with one.

I cannot thank you enough for everything you've done for me. And please know that I believe myself obliged to you.

Give my love and best wishes to your family, and take care of yourself.

Fiona

Jamilyn! He gnashed his teeth. How had she acquired knowledge of Fiona's reputation in Queenston?

He folded the letter. That was inconsequential. He couldn't lose another moment pondering such things. He needed to find Fiona, bring her home, and reconcile this bedlam once and for all.

"I need to find Jamilyn. Now." He eyed his parents and Blair. "She's sent Fiona to Boston under false pretenses."

His jaw clenched. Fiona thought she brought him shame. Nothing could be further from the truth. She had saved him—from that battlefield, and from a life without love, for he had absolutely fallen in love with her all

over again. She was the only woman he
had ever loved and would ever love.

Blair cocked an eyebrow. "Care to
explain?"

"Here, read this." He handed him
the letter. "Jamilyn has gone too
far."

"I feared as much." His mother
crossed her arms. "I didn't wish to
believe her capable of such a misdeed,
but I suspect her desire to separate
you from Fiona outshone her
conscience."

"I believe you're correct." He
rubbed the back of his neck. "I ought
to have noticed it sooner. She was
unduly eager to help Fiona obtain work
in Boston."

Blair finished reading the
letter. "You believe Jamilyn is in
love with you?"

"Aye." His heart ached for Cole.

His cousin shook his head. "Cole
shall be hurt by this." He handed the
letter back.

"Undoubtedly. However, he must
know of this. But first, I must
ascertain Fiona's whereabouts." He

turned toward his carriage. "And that information lies at Jamilyn's house."

"I shall accompany you." Blair followed.

"Don't browbeat her," his father warned.

His mother chased after them. "Aye. Once she realizes you intend to pursue Fiona, she shall be mortified."

With a dip of his chin, he braced his shoulder, before the dust swirled around them, and they rode to Jamilyn's house.

"Allow me to proceed alone," Blair insisted.

"That's probably best." Lachlan sat in the carriage and waited. He had calmed himself enough to pray, and before long, his cousin strode out of Jamilyn's house.

"In her father's presence, Jamilyn confessed." His cousin shook his head. "Pastor West was more than astounded and gravely disappointed, but I'm confident he shall deal with this matter." He glanced back at the wooden house. "She claimed a friend in Queenston divulged the information about Fiona." He offered him a piece of paper. "This is her uncle's address. However, if you hurry, you may catch her coach before she arrives in Boston."

He hesitated. "But, Cole—"

"I shall speak with him directly." His cousin stepped away from the carriage. "Go. Get Fiona back."

*   *   *

Fiona watched the scenery pass by in a blur as the coach bustled down a well-worn road. Each dip, bump and jerk jostled her thoroughly, and further expanded her morose.

At least her stomach no longer growled, a testament to their stop at that inn for some dinner. She appreciated the nourishment, but her thoughts remained in New Callander.

By now, Lachlan must have read her letter. Had her secret, early departure saddened him or angered him? Would he continue to care for Scolty? She caressed the quilt he had given her. If only, she sighed.

A blast charged through the air.

She froze at the familiar sound. Not only had her reputation followed her here, but she couldn't escape the war either. The sounds of musket shots and cannon fire echoed in her mind.

The coach stopped.

She clutched the quilt and counted. Thirteen volleys whizzed by.

"Miss Robertson." Her driver opened the door. She sucked in a breath. "You may as well leave the coach." He offered her his hand. "We shall not be proceeding for a long while."

She didn't move. "Who fired their weapons?"

The driver chuckled. "You needn't be frightened. We're simply blocked by an Independence Day celebration. Those shots were a salute."

She smiled sheepishly and took the man's hand. Every building in this town was decorated in red, blue and white bunting. People lined both sides of the road. She heard the fifers and drummers long before they joined the parade.

"There's naught we can do, but wait for the festivities to dissipate."

"Aye. Thank you. I shall be fine on my own. Please, enjoy yourself. We shall meet back at the coach when the road is passable." The driver tipped his hat and walked into the throng of people, at once lost in the commotion.

She ambled along the outskirts, her mood incongruous with all the merrymaking that surrounded her. This day held no connection to independence for her. By nightfall, she would become a horse groomer and lose all the independence she had ever known.

Finally, she procured a place to stand away from the revellers. The fifers and drummers marched down the road, playing the Chain Cotillion. The lively tune elicited waves and cheers.

Families laughed together, friends played, bonds and memories were formed. She however, stood entirely alone. She hugged herself and peered across the road.

Lachlan's face smiled before her. She shook her head and squeezed her eyes tight. *Wonderful*. Now she had

succumbed to imagining things. She opened her eyes, half-hopeful she'd see him again on the other side of the road. He wasn't there.
She bowed her head and abandoned the line of spectators to wander back to the coach.

"Fiona." She heard her name called. *Impossible.* Her driver only knew her surname. Another Fiona must be amongst the crowd. She walked on.

"Fiona." She heard her name called again. Why hadn't the other Fiona answered? She glanced back in search of an explanation.

The air evacuated her lungs.

She stopped and stared.

Her heart swelled in her chest.

"Lachlan?" she muttered, and blinked rapidly to ensure she did indeed behold the tall, strong, kind man before her. "Lachlan." Her eyes held his. "Why are you not in New Callander?"

"I should think it obvious." His lips curled. "Because you're not there." Her heart fluttered. "I read your letter and had to speak with you." His brown eyes danced. "I do

wish for your dog to remain with me."
He took her hand in his. "However,
that's not all I desire." The warmth
of his fingers flamed through her. Her
knees weakened and her feet tingled.
"I long for you to be a Quarter Horse
breeder. That's the reason I acquired
the mare, and my grandparents insist
on bestowing you with a stallion. Your
family's old home also belongs to you,
because I was the one who purchased
it."

She gasped at each revelation.
This was too much. More than she could
have ever dreamed.

"Come home with me." He kissed
her hand and bent down on one knee. "I
love you, Fiona Robertson. I always
have and I always shall." Her hand
shook in his gentle grip. "Marry me?"

She opened her mouth. Being
Lachlan's wife was all she wanted, all
she needed. She yearned to accept him.
But she couldn't.

She pulled her hand away and
turned her back to him.

F iona's stomach twisted. "I cannot marry you, Lachlan," she forced herself to utter those dreaded words, even though they grated her heart.

"Why ever not?" He bounded in front of her, all happiness drained from his features.

"Did you not understand my letter? I shall bring disgrace upon you, and you don't deserve that."

"Neither do you." He narrowed the space between them and took her hand. "The reputation you gained in Queenston was false and unjust. Anyone who believes those things cannot possibly know you in the slightest. You ought to never have been shamed into leaving." He kissed her hand.

"I fled to keep you from harm. I shan't see you scorned because of me." Tears welled in her eyes.

"You could never defame me. On the contrary, you elevate me. I didn't realize how devoid of meaning and happiness my life had become until I discovered you on your homestead. 'Tis as if you breathed new life into me."

"But, what will people think?"

"No one thinks badly of you." He caressed her cheek. "Jamilyn, on the other hand, has amends to make. I fear she hurt you in an effort to secure me."

She shook her head. "But people at church this morning, and last night at the dance, they gossiped about us."

His smile grew. "I believe I'm to blame for that. I planned to ask you to marry me after church, and my secret didn't remain a secret." He knelt down on one knee again. "Fiona Robertson, I love you with all that I am. I always have. And I believe God intended us to be husband and wife. I've thought that ever since we were young. I'm convinced He sent me to your homestead to provide us with a second chance." His thumb stroked her hand. "Fiona, love of my life, will you marry me?"

Her body quivered. "Aye, Lachlan. I shall marry you." Her tears escaped. He wiped them after he stood. "Lachlan—" she peered deep into eyes that reflected her feelings perfectly "—I love you." She wrapped her arms about his neck. "You did more than capture my homestead, you captured my heart. And it shall be yours forever."

He wrapped his good arm around her waist. "I've dreamed of this my entire life."

She laughed, as anticipation caused her heart to skip. "Then I do believe we ought not to wait any longer. We must begin living our dreams."

"We definitely shall." His lips touched hers and from that moment on their dreams flowered.

Please enjoy the other books in the

HIGHLAND HEARTS IN THE AMERICAS

Series

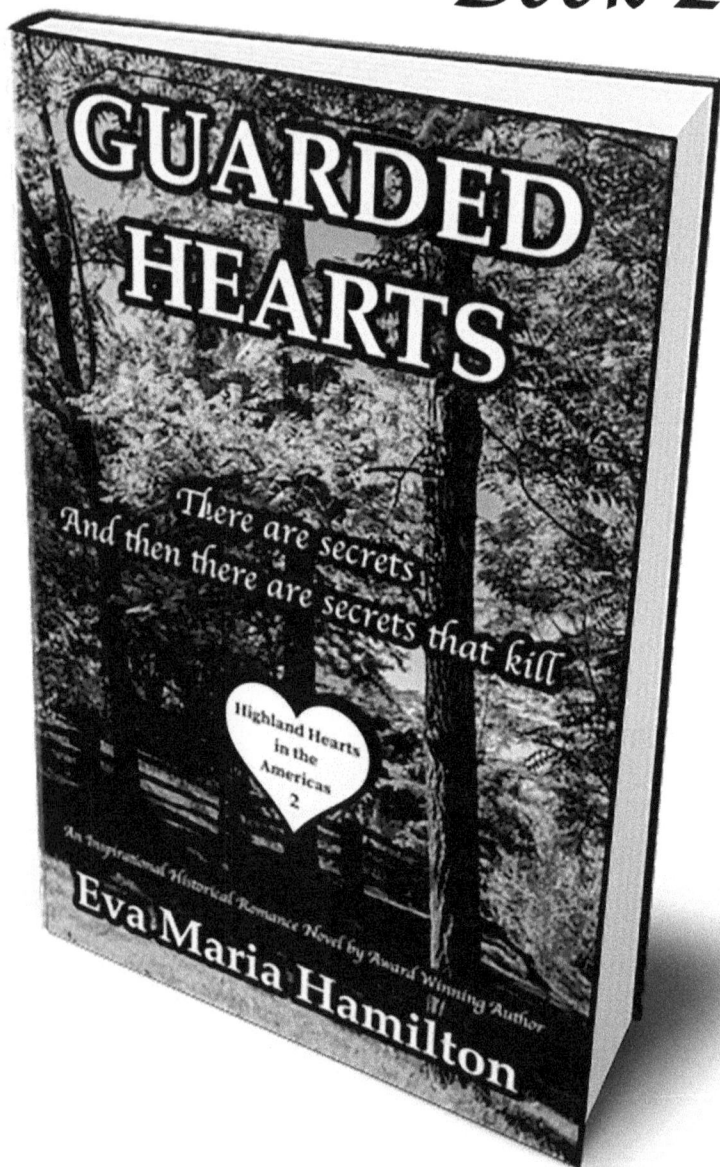

Book 2

GUARDED HEARTS

There are secrets,
And then there are secrets that kill

Highland Hearts
in the
Americas
2

An Inspirational Historical Romance Novel by Award Winning Author

Eva Maria Hamilton

On a secret mission, Penelope
Sherwood is in enemy territory
in the Mohawk Valley of the
United States during the War of
1812. She's willing to risk
death to fulfill her late
father's dying request, but she
never expected to risk her
heart.

Meeting Blair McAllister was not
part of the plan. If he found
out her secret she could be
killed.

But what secret is he hiding?

GUARDED HEARTS

There are secrets
And then there are secrets that kill

Highland Hearts
in the
Americas
2

An Inspirational Historical Romance Novel by Award Winning Author

Eva Maria Hamilton

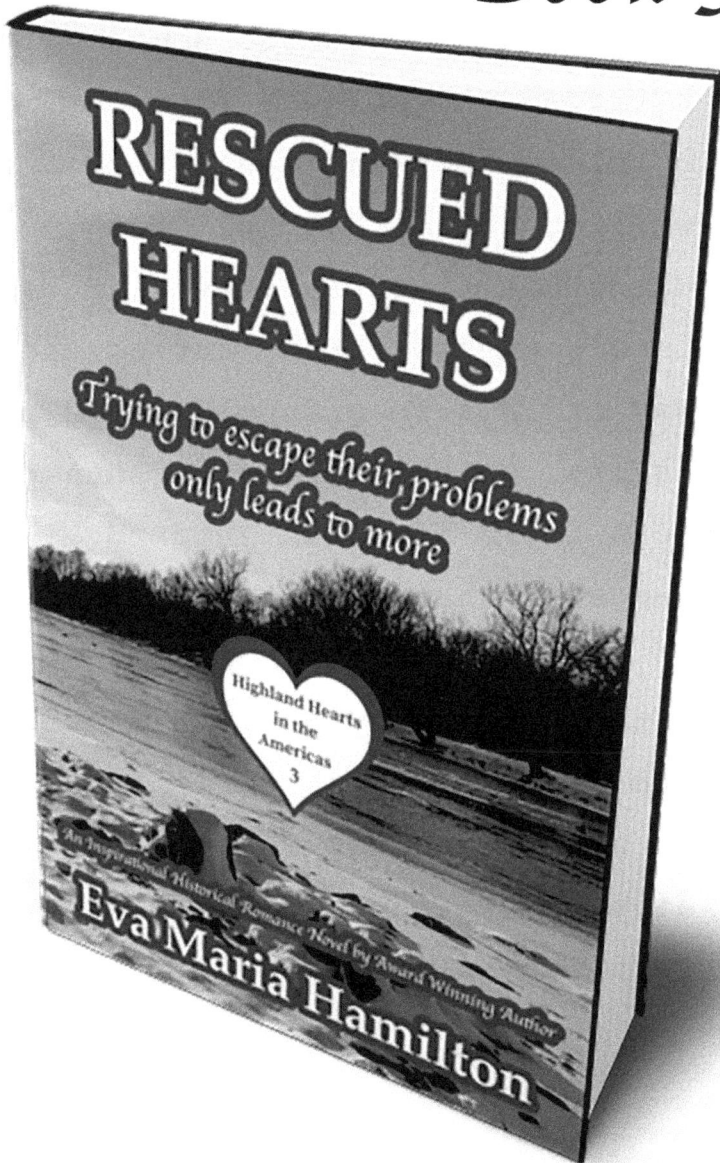

Book 3

RESCUED HEARTS

Trying to escape their problems only leads to more

Highland Hearts in the Americas 3

An Inspirational Historical Romance Novel by Award Winning Author

Eva Maria Hamilton

Jamilyn West switched homes with a friend to get away from her problems. But one man is not willing to let her go. Cole Munro has secretly travelled into enemy territory during the War of 1812 to ensure Jamilyn's safety. But his presence puts both their lives in jeopardy. And even though he has no desire to return to their hometown either, they may have no other choice but to risk their lives in an escape that leads them directly to the trouble they left behind.

RESCUED HEARTS

*Trying to escape their problems
only leads to more*

Highland Hearts
in the
Americas
3

An Inspirational Historical Romance Novel by Award Winning Author

Eva Maria Hamilton

Dear Reader,

I hope you enjoyed Captured Hearts!

This book, and series, was originally being considered for Harlequin's Heartsong Presents line, but unfortunately that line closed. That was over a decade ago and Lachlan and Fiona have been living with me ever since. I have rewritten and edited this book, and series, so many times over the years. But I am finally happy to release them out into the world and let others fall in love with the people of New Callander and enjoy the characters as much as I have.

Just as the characters in the book do, I pray that you also know unconditional love and are always surrounded by amazing people.

If you liked Lachlan and Fiona's story, please leave a review, they mean the world to me.

And please also connect with me.

I look forward to meeting you and staying in touch!

Sincerely,

Eva Maria Hamilton

About the Author

Eva Maria Hamilton spent years studying people from all different areas of academia and brings that understanding of the human condition into each of her written pieces. An advocate for lifelong learning, Eva Maria Hamilton studied in both Canada and the United States, earning a diploma in Human Resources Management, a Bachelor of Arts degree in Psychology, an Honours Bachelor of Arts Degree in History, and a Master of Science in Education. She homeschooled her oldest daughter who is now in university, and still homeschools her youngest daughter, along with their two collies, while acting as Co-CEO in her Co-founded business, TestLauncher.

Eva Maria Hamilton is the author of Highland Hearts, a Love Inspired Historical novel published by Harlequin. Her novel, Highland Hearts:

- **Won 2nd Place in the Heart of Excellence, Reader's Choice Contest - Historical Romance Category**

- **Won 2nd Place in the Heart of Excellence, Reader's Choice Contest - Inspirational/Traditional Romance Category**

- Was an **Inspirational Series Finalist in the 2013 Gayle Wilson Award of Excellence**

Eva Maria Hamilton is also the owner of Lilac Lane Publishing, which has published a series of Jane Austen Colouring & Activity Books.

Her compilation book, The Ultimate Collection of Jane Austen's Colouring and Activity Books: With More Than 240 Activities And Over 250 Illustrations from 1875-1906:

- Won the 2024 International Impact Book Awards.

Connect with the Author

To discover other books
Eva Maria Hamilton
has published, or soon will,
please visit her online:

EMAIL:
EvaMariaHamilton@gmail.com

FACEBOOK: Eva Maria Hamilton

FACEBOOK: Lilac Lane Publishing

X / TWITTER: @HamiltonEvaM

LINKEDIN: Eva Maria Hamilton

AMAZON.com: Amazon Author

AMAZON.ca: Amazon Author

LILAC LANE PUBLISHING:
www.LilacLanePublishing.com

WEBSITE:
www.EvaMariaHamilton.com

The Award Winning Book That Started It All

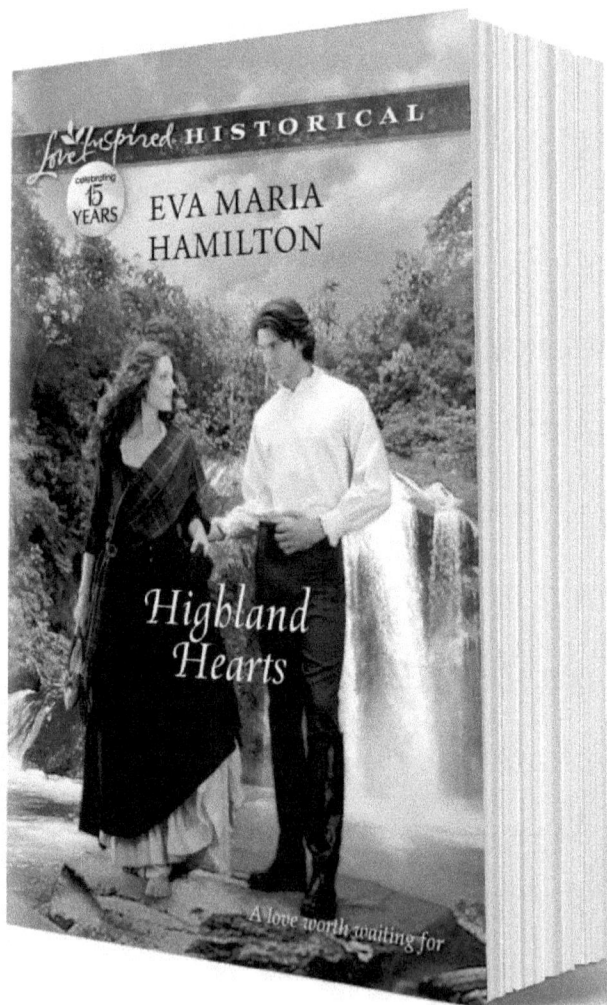

Love Inspired HISTORICAL

celebrating 15 YEARS

EVA MARIA HAMILTON

Highland Hearts

A love worth waiting for

Highland Hearts

Scotland 1748

The Battle of Culloden is over,
but one Highlander's fight has
just begun — Logan McAllister
survived years of indentured
servitude in the Americas to
reach this moment. Now he's
returned to Scotland, ready to
redeem the secret promise from
Sheena Montgomery's father —
that his years as a servant
would earn him Sheena's hand in
marriage. But when he arrives
home, he learns that Sheena's
father has died, his contract
has been lost — and Sheena is
engaged to another man.

"A good story that shows the lifestyles and prejudices that prevailed in 18th-century Scotland..."
Romantic Times

"Fascinating Scottish Romance...

Can't wait for more from this author."
5 Star Reviewer

"A great story about an interesting period...I look forward to reading more books by this new author."
5 Star Reviewer

"I found this to be a wonderful book...Highly recommend this book."
5 Star Reviewer

"An edge of your seat romance! Excellent! Loved it!"
5 Star Reviewer

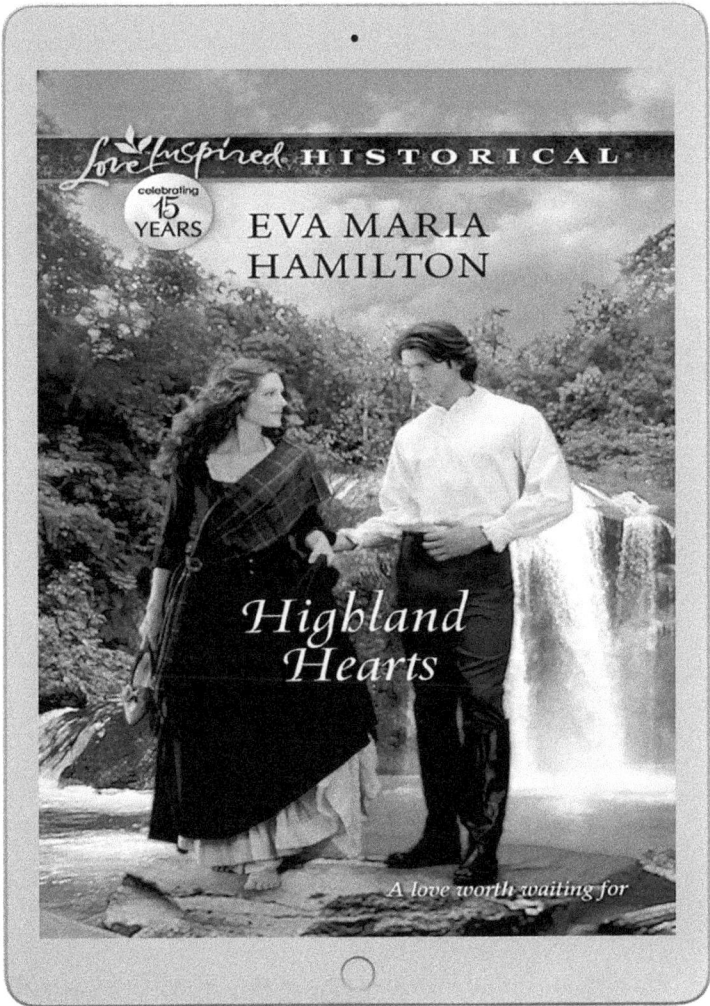

EVA MARIA
HAMILTON

Highland
Hearts

A love worth waiting for

Please Also Enjoy:

DISINHERITED LOVE

A Short Inspirational
Historical Romance Story
from Award Winning Author

Eva Maria Hamilton

England 1795
An elopement in Gretna Green
seems like the perfect solution,
but for these star-crossed lovers
trouble finds them first

Disinherited Love

Lily Chrisson and Lord Gavin Mackenzie hail from very different classes; a serious problem for those in love during Regency England. And yet, they're en route to secretly marry in Gretna Green. That is, until she discovers the truth. Torn apart, his determination wars with her principles, and family with even more secrets emerge in this redeeming short story.

Jane Austen's
Pride And Prejudice
Colouring & Activity Book

By Eva Maria Hamilton

Featuring Illustrations from 1895

Step into the world
of Jane Austen!

Immerse yourself in colouring 40 illustrations from the 1895 edition of Pride and Prejudice.

Enjoy 40 activities, such as Matching Characters to Quotes, Search Words, Anagrams, and more.

Have fun in the Regency Era!

"...If you are a fan of Pride and Prejudice you will love this book. The illustrations are wonderful and the activities are engaging."
5 Star Reviewer

**Rated
5 Stars
On
Amazon
★★★★★**

Jane Austen's Sense And Sensibility Colouring & Activity Book

By: Eva Maria Hamilton

Featuring Illustrations from 1896

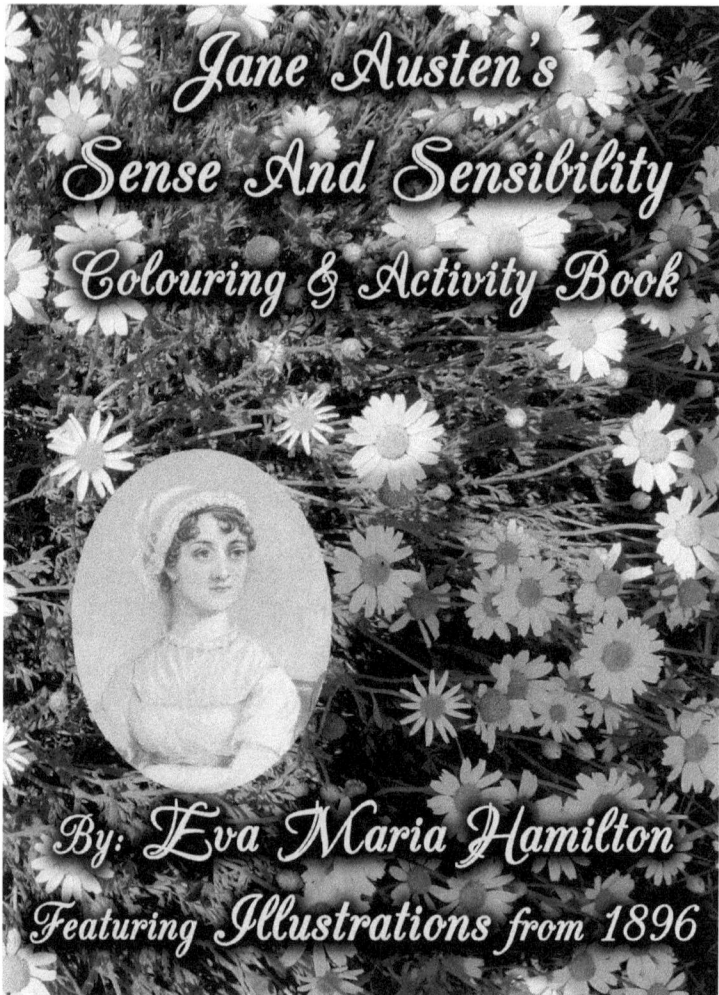

Step into the world
of Jane Austen!

Immerse yourself in colouring 40 illustrations from the 1896 edition of Sense and Sensibility.

Enjoy 40 activities, such as Matching Characters to Quotes, Search Words, Anagrams, and more.

Have fun in the Regency Era!

Rated
5 Stars
On
Amazon
★★★★★

Jane Austen's
Emma
Colouring & Activity Book

By: Eva Maria Hamilton

Featuring Illustrations from 1896

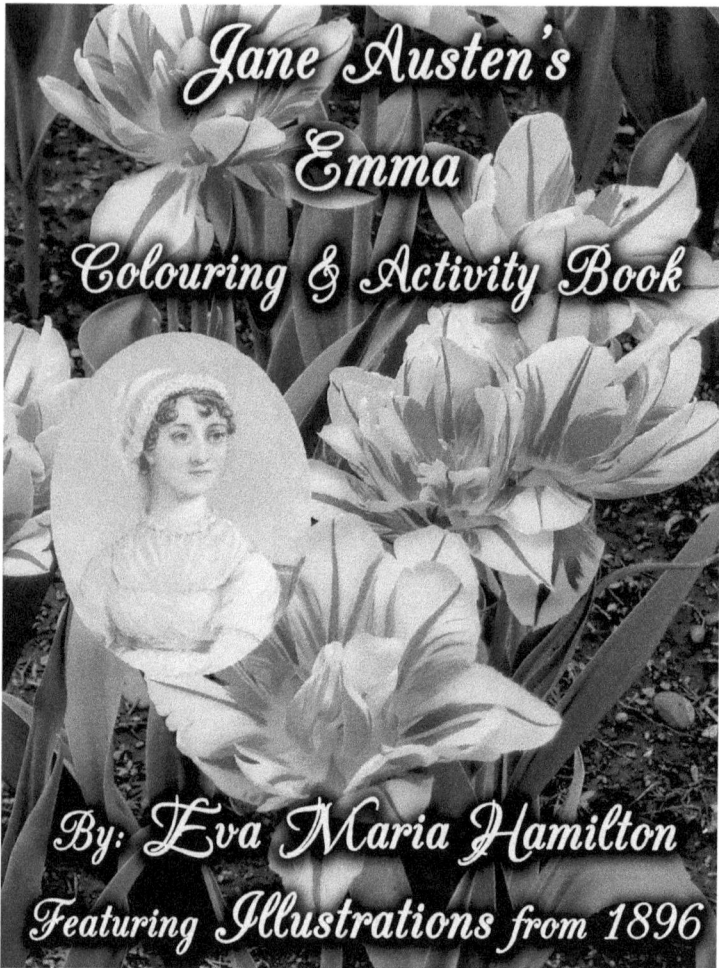

Step into the world
of Jane Austen!

Immerse yourself in
colouring 40 illustrations
from the 1896 edition of
Emma.

Enjoy 40 activities, such
as Matching Characters to
Quotes, Search Words,
Anagrams, and more.

Have fun in the Regency
Era!

*"Beautifully presented...
Lovely as a gift."*
Reviewer

Rated
5 Stars
On
Amazon
★★★★★

Jane Austen's Persuasion Colouring & Activity Book

By: Eva Maria Hamilton

Featuring Illustrations from 1897

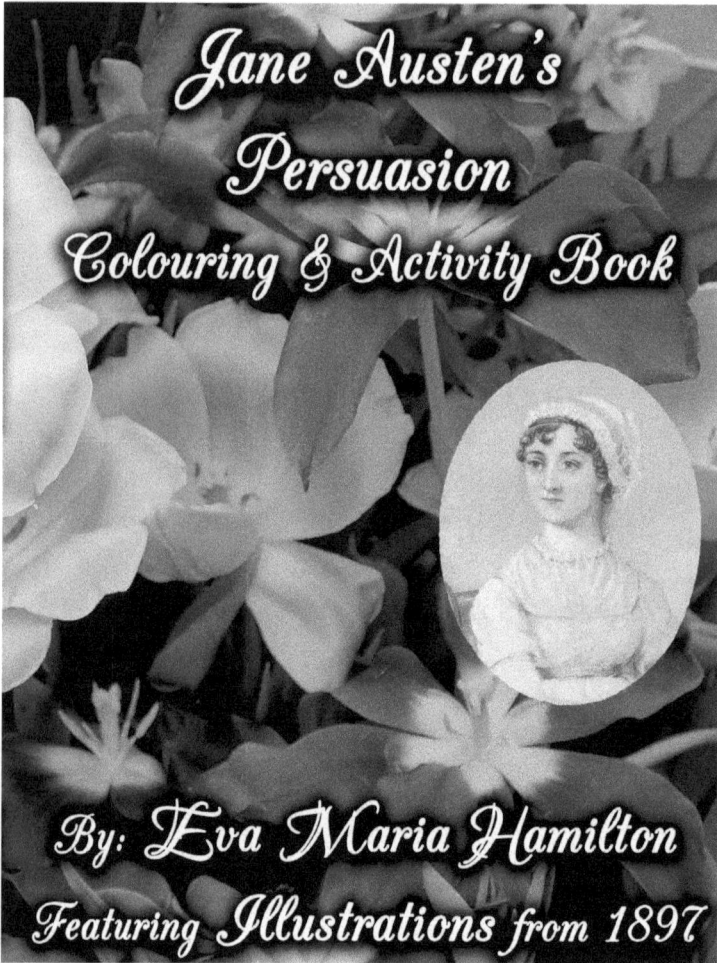

Step into the world
of Jane Austen!

Immerse yourself in colouring 20 illustrations from the 1897 edition of Persuasion.

Enjoy 20 activities, such as Matching Characters to Quotes, Search Words, Anagrams, and more.

Have fun in the Regency Era!

"Very educational... Very beautiful."

Reviewer

**Rated
5 Stars
On
Goodreads
★★★★★**

Jane Austen's Mansfield Park Colouring & Activity Book

By: Eva Maria Hamilton

Featuring Illustrations from 1897

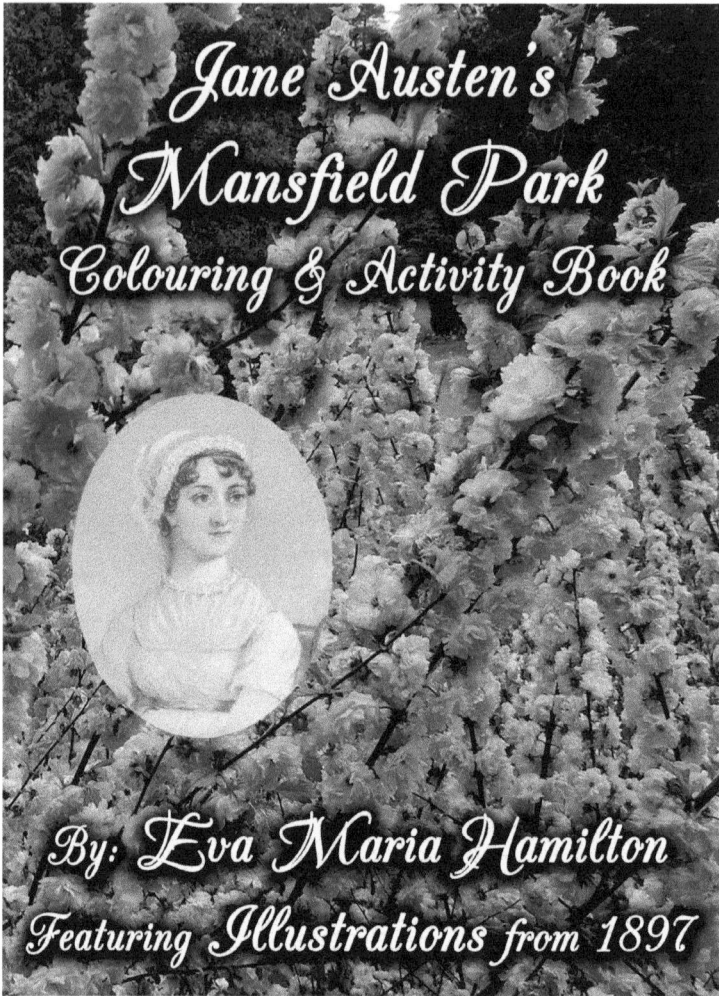

Step into the world of Jane Austen!

Immerse yourself in colouring 40 illustrations from the 1897 edition of Mansfield Park, plus 7 bonus illustrations from the 1875 edition.

Enjoy 47 activities, such as Matching Characters to Quotes, Search Words, Anagrams, and more.

Have fun in the Regency Era!

Rated
5 Stars
On
Amazon
★★★★★

Jane Austen's
Northanger Abbey
Colouring & Activity Book

By: Eva Maria Hamilton

Featuring Illustrations from 1897

Step into the world
of Jane Austen!

Immerse yourself in colouring 20 illustrations from the 1897 edition of Northanger Abbey.

Enjoy 20 activities, such as Matching Characters to Quotes, Search Words, Anagrams, and more.

Have fun in the Regency Era!

Rated
5 Stars
On
Amazon
and
Goodreads
★★★★★

The Ultimate Collection

All 6 Books in 1 Plus More

of Jane Austen's

Colouring & Activity Books

Pride & Prejudice

Sense & Sensibility

Emma

Mansfield Park

Persuasion

Northanger Abbey

Plus Bonus Illustrations, and Activities From Her Other Writings:
Sandition, Lady Susan, The Watsons, Letters, and more.

By: Eva Maria Hamilton

With More Than 240 Activities
And Over 250 Illustrations from 1875-1906

The Ultimate Collection
of Jane Austen's
Colouring and Activity
Books, including:
Pride and Prejudice,
Sense and Sensibility,
Emma,
Mansfield Park,
Persuasion, and
Northanger Abbey.

Plus bonus
illustrations
and activities
from her other
writings:
Sandition,
Lady Susan,
The Watsons,
Letters,
and more.

With more than
240 activities
and over 250
illustrations
from 1875-1906!

INTERNATIONAL
IMPACT
BOOK AWARDS

Milton Keynes UK
Ingram Content Group UK Ltd.
UKHW040034141124
2824UKWH00001B/19

9 781068 990700